# THE BABY
## ON MY
# DOORSTEP

## BOOKS BY MIRANDA SMITH

*Some Days Are Dark*

*What I Know*

*The One Before*

*Not My Mother*

*His Loving Wife*

*The Killer's Family*

*The Family Home*

*The School Trip*

*The Weekend Away*

*The Writer*

*Loving Mothers*

*Did You See Evie?*

# THE BABY
## ON MY
# DOORSTEP

MIRANDA SMITH

bookouture

Published by Bookouture in 2025

An imprint of Storyfire Ltd.
Carmelite House
50 Victoria Embankment
London EC4Y 0DZ

www.bookouture.com

The authorised representative in the EEA is Hachette Ireland
8 Castlecourt Centre
Dublin 15 D15 XTP3
Ireland
(email: info@hbgi.ie)

ISBN: 978-1-83618-901-5
eBook ISBN: 978-1-83618-900-8

*For Whitney*

# ONE

My divorce papers sit on the kitchen countertop.

I attempt to pour another glass of wine, but the bottle is empty.

Great. I'm a sad stereotype, on the verge of drunkenness, my marriage in ruins. And alone. Can't forget that part.

I pick up my phone to call Vivienne, my best friend, but she doesn't answer. I can't say I blame her. She's listened to me enough this past year. I shoot over a text instead.

*Divorce papers arrived. Want to get drunk?*

I snicker at the cheekiness of the message, but only for a second. Her response doesn't come in right away, and I'm back to the loneliness.

Most of Byron's things are still here. What started as a few nights at his friend's house turned into an extended stay at a hotel. Last month, he officially moved into his brother's old apartment. Once a week, he returns home to do laundry and collect more of his belongings, dragging out the process of fully moving out as long as possible. The end of our marriage doesn't seem true if all his belongings remain in the house. His pool table and golf clubs and cracked leather sofa.

But our divorce is real. The stack of papers on the counter proves it.

Where did we go wrong? What ruined us?

The answer is simple and complicated all at once.

Another woman, although probably not in the way you think. It wasn't some illicit affair that wrecked our marriage.

Erin, my younger sister, was murdered more than a year ago, taking with her any semblance of happiness in my own life, stripping away all the good things about me like sandpaper against wood. Her case remains unresolved, and in my desperation to prove what happened to her, I've become a shell of myself.

The last time I saw her plays on repeat in my mind.

We met for dinner at our favorite restaurant, chowing down on a platter of green salad drenched in parmesan dressing and shrimp alla vodka pasta. The wine was flowing. Smiles wide. Lungs hurting from all the laughter. The world always felt right when we were together.

It was an all-round perfect night. Until Adam arrived. Her ex-boyfriend.

He approached our table just after we'd ordered dessert, his presence a dark storm cloud interrupting a bright summer day. At first, I thought he'd followed her; he was controlling when they were together, even more so in the months since they'd split. The moment Erin laid eyes on him, her demeanor changed, her shoulders raising as though she were closing into herself. When he bent down to hug her, she accepted his embrace. He wasn't there by coincidence. She'd invited him.

"What are you doing here?" I asked, my words infused with anger.

"Erin and I have plans," he said, never once taking his eyes off her. He refused to look at me, and I wonder, now, if it's because he knew what was going to happen next, if he was already aware of the violence to come.

"It's fine, Emily. We made plans for later." She looked at Adam, suddenly seeming smaller, almost cowering. "We were just about to have dessert. Please, just wait in the car."

He checks the time on his wristwatch and stomps his feet.

"Ten minutes," he says, before turning on his heels.

I watched as he weaved between the tables on the patio, my anger spiking.

"Sorry about that," Erin says.

"You said the two of you broke up."

"We did," Erin said, the vibrancy from earlier gone. "He's only here as a friend."

"Don't lie to me. Exes can't be friends." My eyes cut toward him. "Especially after everything he put you through."

Adam was a heavy drinker. Alcohol made him more aggressive, more paranoid. Erin always claimed he never hit her, but the shouting arguments I overheard were bad enough. They reminded me of the worst moments from our childhood.

"He's getting better," she said.

"Do you know how ridiculous you sound?" My tone was more belittling than I'd meant. "How many times did Mom get better over the years?"

That comment went too far. I shouldn't have weaponized our shared childhood against her, but at the same time, I couldn't fathom why my sister was being so stupid. Once a drunk, always a drunk. People like our mother, like Adam, don't change.

"You need to trust me." She raised her chin. "I know what I'm doing."

"If you want me to trust you, stop making stupid choices." I stood, dropping cash on the table. Maybe I was the one who'd had too much to drink, the alcohol feeding my anger. Or maybe I was tired of Erin being so irresponsible.

"Please, Emily."

Erin got up and wrapped her arms around me, squeezing me tighter than usual. I sensed then something was off, that something sinister had interrupted our evening, and it had been ushered in by Adam. Or maybe, I think with a shiver, I've added these sentimental elements to my memory over time.

Either way, my anger made me defiant. I left without saying another word. If I'd known that would be the last time I saw her, I would have done everything differently.

In my darkest moments, I imagine what happened to her after I left that night. I imagine a disparaged Erin leaning on Adam for comfort. Perhaps whatever plans they made were thwarted, and the two of them decided to continue drinking instead. Adam is always at his worst when he drinks. Maybe Erin did something to offend him, said the wrong thing. It would be minor in the eyes of a normal person, of course, but for someone like Adam, insecure and egotistical, fueled by alcohol and simmering resentment, it could have sent him into a rage.

I imagine him hitting her, pushing her and causing her to strike her head. I imagine his hands closing around her throat. Afterwards, I believe he drove her out into the woods, placing her lifeless body in a place it may never be found.

He killed her that night, and it's possible my argument with her was the first fallen domino in a series of unfortunate events. I'll always blame myself for that.

My eyes clench shut as the beginning waves of a migraine roll in.

I wish Erin were still here. I wish I hadn't ruined things with Byron. I wish Viv would answer the phone. I wish I had someone—

There's a knock at the door, the sound so unexpected I drop my wine glass. Thankfully, it falls from the sofa to the plush rug without shattering. One less mess to clean.

"Hello?" I call from the living room, loud enough that

whoever is standing on the front porch should be able to hear. I reach for my phone, looking to see if Vivienne has responded. She hasn't, and even if she was coming over, she couldn't have arrived this quickly.

Stumbling to my feet, I begin walking to the foyer.

"Who is it?" I ask again, this time certain whoever is there can hear me.

Our house is the last one on a long stretch of road heading towards the woods and distant lake. Byron comes and goes as he pleases, but he almost always messages me first. And the Uber Eats driver that delivered my takeout Chinese food left more than an hour ago.

The second knock—a forceful pounding—sends a shiver down my spine.

It's dark outside. Not exactly the middle of the night, but too late for door-to-door salesmen. No neighbors live within walking distance. No one with honest intentions would continue to knock without identifying themselves.

There's a small window to the left of the door that provides a clear view of the driveway. The only car outside belongs to me. Byron's car isn't there, nor anyone else's.

If someone is knocking on my front door, how did they get here? And why won't they—

Fear rattles through me at the sound of the third knock.

"I'm calling the police," I shout, my cell phone already in hand. I'm not sure what their response will be to someone appearing at my doorstep and refusing to respond. Probably not much, but I'm hoping the threat will coax the visitor into talking.

Instead, I hear the unmistakable sound of footsteps retreating. Out the window, I see the bushes in the front yard rustle, proof of some passing movement, but by the time I reposition myself to look from a different angle, whoever brushed by them is gone. No one is there. They knocked and left, but why?

There's no way in hell I'm opening that door. I've read too many scary books, not to mention what happened to my own sister.

My heart thumps inside my chest, the room unbearably cold as fear wraps around me, making it difficult to breathe.

I put my ear against the door, listening. Maybe the person will come back. Maybe a second person is there waiting. Maybe Byron or Viv will call, wondering why I'm being so weird and refusing to answer the door.

The sound that greets my ears is the last one I would have ever expected.

It's a nasal, high-pitched wailing. The undeniable cry of an infant.

Dread runs through me, forcing my brain into overdrive but compelling my body to keep still. Am I hearing what I think I'm hearing? Could it be some kind of animal? A racoon or a squirrel? Those sound nothing like babies, I know, but would be far more predictable to show up on my porch late at night. Not a child. A baby!

Maybe I've had too much to drink, I think, still grasping for logic. This could all be some auditory hallucination. But another wail rings out, proving that theory wrong. There's definitely a crying child on the other side of the door.

My hand goes to the doorknob but stops. Could this be some kind of trap? Didn't I read about some ruse serial killers have? Coming up with fiendish ways to make vulnerable women open their doors. *You're not overreacting*, my brain tells me. *Your own sister went missing. She was likely murdered...*

I return to the kitchen, sliding a knife from the cutting block, just in case. The odds of two sisters being murdered in separate incidents must be slim, but you can never be too careful.

One hand grips the knife, as the other twists the doorknob.

The view in front of me is familiar, unremarkable. Our

faded picket fence, the metal mailbox, dying flowers lining the walkway. There doesn't appear to be anyone waiting in the shadows. Two glowing taillights appear in the distance, getting smaller with each passing second.

I look down.

A carrier sits on our welcome mat, a patterned blanket draped over it, preventing me from seeing what's inside.

Another cry breaks through the night, and I'm startled by how close it sounds now that there isn't a barrier between us.

I bend down, lifting the blanket with shaking hands.

A baby stares back at me, eyes wide and wet, cheeks red from all the crying. Its little feet move back and forth, trying and failing to run away.

"What the hell?"

I reach forward, touching the infant's warm body, feeling it wiggle.

It cries louder, and I wonder if it—he or she—is as confused as I am.

I struggle to unfasten the chest strap keeping the child in place. As I lift its little body, I'm afraid my touch will do more harm than good—I've not held a baby since Erin was born.

"You're going to be okay," I say, those maternal instincts coming back to me sooner than I would have expected, just as another morbid thought enters my brain:

*At least you're no longer alone.*

# TWO

I hold the phone in the crook of my neck and shoulder, using both arms to try and comfort the baby, rocking it gently. It hasn't stopped crying since I opened the door.

The 911 operator asks standard questions. What's my name? My location? Does the child appear to be injured or malnourished?

"It won't stop screaming," I say, pleading for help. The operator's responses fill one ear, while the baby's yells cloud the other.

"Is there a safe area where you can put the child down?" she says. "We need you to inspect it so we know what medical assistance to provide."

"Can't they do that when they get here?" I ask. Again, it's been decades since I cared for an infant; I was only a child then myself. Interacting with this baby is like trying to have a conversation with someone who speaks another language. No matter what I do, we're not understanding each other.

"We need to know what type of help to send," the operator says.

Exhaling, I place the baby on the sofa, watching as its arms and legs writhe around. There's a sheep design on the zip-up jumper that I hadn't noticed before.

"Do you see any obvious wounds? Any bleeding?"

"No," I say, relieved.

"Unzip the onesie," she says. "Let us know if you see anything abnormal."

Ten minutes ago I was alone, drowning in my own sorrows. Now I'm undressing an infant in the middle of my living room. Everything feels surreal, wrong. I see a taut belly and outward facing bellybutton. The child seems perfectly healthy. I rub its chest, which shudders with every sharp intake of breath.

"I don't see any wounds," I tell the woman. "It looks fine, it just won't stop crying!"

"Is the child male or female?"

I peek inside the diaper. "It's a girl."

Saying those words, I'm brought back to my own childhood. My earliest memory is my mother bringing Erin home when I was seven. She said those same words, and my chest filled with excitement. A sister. My own real-life doll to play with and spoil and protect.

"Police are en route," she says, listing off other instructions. The formality of her orders disintegrates the happy memories in my head.

"Oh my goodness," I say in disbelief.

"What is it?"

"It stopped crying." I correct myself, lowering my voice. "*She* stopped crying. It looks like she's about to fall asleep."

Moments later, the police arrive. They run to the baby, giving her their own inspection. A uniformed officer remains with me in the living room, asking me detailed questions about how the child ended up with me. Unfortunately, there isn't much information to give. I'd had no warning—other than those mystery knocks—and the next thing I know there was a baby on my doorstep.

"Emily?" A woman with thick curly hair cropped to her shoulders approaches me, holding out a hand. "I'm Tabitha. I work for the Department of Children's Services. I'm a social worker." Her eyes wash over me, then inspect the rest of the room. "It looks like you've had one hell of a night."

"Tell me about it."

I sit on the sofa, watching as the officers and paramedics lay the baby back down in the carrier and take her outside. There's an immediate sense of relief, knowing the child is now in safe hands, but a storm of confusion remains. How did she end up here? Who on earth would leave their baby on a stranger's doorstep?

"I have just a few routine questions," she says, "and then we'll be out of your hair."

We go over the same limited information I've already told the phone operator and the responding officers. Tabitha writes down everything I say in a green spiral notebook.

"Paramedics said she looks healthy," she says. "I'm happy you were able to act so quickly."

The possible danger of the situation disturbs me. What if the child had been left at a different house? What if someone hadn't been home and she was left crying for hours? Days? What if the person who answered the door had been a threat?

"I'm still in shock," I say. "I mean, I've read stories about people leaving their babies in bathrooms or dumpsters, but I never thought I'd see it. Why on earth would someone leave their child at a stranger's house?"

Tabitha sighs. "Thankfully, it's not a regular occurrence. Unfortunately, with the recent restrictions on reproductive rights, there's been an uptick in this sort of thing. My guess is whoever had the child was on their way to the fire station down the road, but stopped here instead."

I've read about that, too. Fire stations are meant to be infant safety drop-off centers. Parents can leave their baby there, no

questions asked, a safer alternative than abandoning them altogether. Still, I don't think I've ever heard about that happening
here.

"It is strange, though," Tabitha continues. "Usually we see
newborns being abandoned. This baby looks to be around four
or five months old."

"People are crazy," I say, thinking back to when Erin was
that age. I used to love playing with her, rolling around on the
floor. By the time she was four months old, I could never
remember a life without her. How could someone care for a
child that long and just decide to abandon them?

"One last thing," she says. "Would you volunteer a DNA
sample? It's standard procedure. One of the paramedics can
take a mouth swab before we leave."

"Sure," I say, "if it's necessary."

"We could come back with a warrant." Her tone is informa-
tive, not threatening. "Whenever there's a situation like this
involving a woman in child-bearing years, we run DNA tests to
make sure there isn't a familial connection."

"Of course," I say.

"It'll only take a moment," she says, standing.

As she's walking out the front door to talk to the paramedics, someone else comes running through the door. It's
Byron. He's shaken and out of breath.

"Emily?" His expression softens when he sees me. "Are you
okay?"

"I'm fine," I say, ashamed to admit I'm happy to see him.
This entire situation felt overwhelming on my own. "What are
you doing here?"

"I heard our address over my police scanner," he says. "I
rushed over to make sure you were all right."

"Since when do you have a police scanner?"

"The newspaper suggested I get one for this project I'm

working on," he says. He wraps his arms around me. "I was so scared that something had happened to you."

His embrace feels both familiar and foreign. I'm reminded of the stack of divorce papers still sitting on the kitchen counter. Byron isn't supposed to be the person who comforts me. Not anymore. I pull away, reluctantly, and he takes a step back too.

"Well, something is clearly going on," he says, looking back at the flashing lights streaming into the living room. "Was there a break-in?"

I cross my arms and exhale. "Someone left a baby on our doorstep."

"A baby?"

"Yes."

It feels surreal saying it, even though the past hour of my life has been consumed by this event. Sharing this with Byron is complicated. It wasn't just the grief over Erin's disappearance that drove us apart; my reluctance to have a child proved to be the final nail in our marriage's coffin.

Byron sits on the sofa, shoulders slumped. He looks at home here. Like he belongs. I've seen him sit in this very position countless times, but now it feels odd.

"They think someone just abandoned the baby?"

"Yes," I say. "According to the social worker, it's more common than I realized."

"That's horrible."

I look back at the kitchen. When I catch sight of the divorce papers, I feel like I've been pierced with an arrow. I wonder if Byron has already signed his copy, or if he's dragging his feet like I am.

"The whole thing gave me a scare, but I'm all right."

"Are you sure?"

Before I can answer, Vivienne comes running into the house, her face as perplexed as Byron's was when he arrived, her eyes bouncing between the officers and paramedics visible through the open door.

"What the hell happened?" Her gaze falls on me. "Are you okay?"

"I'm fine," I say. "I'll explain everything."

"I got your message, but I wasn't expecting all this." She takes a step forward but stops when she sees Byron. "Hello, B. Long time no see."

"Just wanted to check on Emily," he says, standing. "I feel better knowing she won't be here alone."

He takes a step forward, as though he's about to kiss me on the cheek, our old goodbye tradition, but he thinks better of it. My chest hurts as he awkwardly shuffles out of the house we once called home. Vivienne and I stand in silence as we watch him leave.

"The divorce papers arrived today," I say. Even though more urgent things have happened since then, it's still fresh in my mind.

"You told me." Vivienne reaches for my arm, rubbing it up and down.

"Ms. March?" Tabitha walks back inside, a uniformed man beside her. He carries a clear Ziplock bag in his hands. "This is one of our paramedics. He's here for the sample we discussed."

I nod, following the man's instructions as he explains how the sample will be collected. It only takes a few seconds, the scratchy end of a Q-tip swiping the inside of my mouth. Viv watches us, a look of confusion on her face.

When the man finishes, he seals up the bag, and turns to leave with Tabitha.

"Wait," I say, chasing after them. I lower my voice. "What will happen to her? The baby."

Tabitha gives a tight smile. "She'll be taken to the hospital to confirm she's as healthy as she looks. Once she's released, she'll be placed in the system. We'll put her with a foster family until we can track down any next of kin."

My insides tense. "That's awful. Just shipping her off to strangers?"

"She's lucky you were here to answer the door. She'll be able to get the help she needs as soon as possible." Tabitha puts her hand on my shoulder. "The police might reach out to you in the next week, if they have any follow-up questions."

"Sure."

An hour ago, I never would have predicted I'd be part of a situation like this. It serves as yet another reminder of how ugly the world can be. Marriages fall apart. Sisters get murdered. Mothers abandon their children on a stranger's doorstep. I recall the knocks I heard before answering the door. What must have been going through that person's mind? Did they feel any remorse over what they were doing, or were they simply relieved to have a little less responsibility?

I cross my arms over my chest as I watch them leave. Vivienne steps closer to me.

"Are you going to tell me what's going on?"

I sigh. "I don't even know where to start."

"I brought wine," she says, holding up a brown paper bag, "if you're still in the mood to get drunk."

The tension in my neck and shoulders begins to melt away. "Thank God."

# THREE

It's difficult to tap into a normal Monday after the weekend I had.

My mind keeps returning to the baby. Is she cared for? Did this experience cause her any harm? Where is the mother? When I'm not thinking about that, I'm thinking about Byron, which inevitably leads to more thoughts about Erin.

In the wake of my sister's death, all I cared about was seeking justice. Finding out exactly what happened to her—and making Adam pay for what he'd done—became more important than anything. My job, my friendships, my marriage. Byron tried to be supportive, but as time passed, he wanted me to move on, something I couldn't do, not when my sister's killer was still walking the streets.

It was that desperate need to find out what happened to Erin that drove a wedge between us. Now, Byron lives in his brother's old apartment across town, our marriage in shambles. With the chaos of the weekend, I never got around to signing the divorce papers.

Luckily, my job doesn't feel like actual work. Maybe that's because Viv, my best friend, doubles as my boss.

Viv and I first met in college. After graduation, I used my English degree to work at a small newspaper, covering the crime beat and local sports. Viv took a loan from her father and started her own digital marketing company. That company has now grown into a multi-million-dollar enterprise. By the end of this year, a second office is expected to open in Denver.

Vivienne was more than happy to hire me on for the company's writing team. I mostly do copywriting, creating the monthly newsletter, and helping on seasonal projects as they come about. Eventually, Erin started working here, too.

"Morning." A voice interrupts my thoughts. I look up from my laptop to see Matt, Vivienne's husband and CFO, standing at my desk. "I heard you had quite the weekend," he says, sipping from his to-go coffee.

"It's crazy, isn't it?" I say, figuring Vivienne has already filled him in on all the details. After the police left, she stayed at my house into the wee hours. We eventually fell asleep on the couch. "I'm happy Viv came over. Gave me a chance to process everything."

"Any word on the kid?"

I shake my head. "The police said they might follow up with some questions, but I haven't heard anything."

"Wild," he says, chewing on a toothpick. "I guess we have our very own hero in the building."

"I wouldn't go that far."

"I would," Viv says. She walks behind Matt, giving him a kiss on the cheek, before looking at me. "What are you even doing here? I told you to take a couple days."

"It's not like anything happened to me. I mean, yeah, the whole experience was shocking and surreal, but it's not like I need to recover from anything."

Truth is, if I were to spend my entire day at home, I'd do nothing but obsess over the divorce. I've been using the entire ordeal with the baby as an excuse to avoid it.

"I'm only going to be in a few hours, anyway," I say, looking back at my computer. "I have that thing later."

"What thing?" Matt asks.

"None of your business," Viv says playfully, squeezing his shoulder before he walks away. She steps closer, lowering her voice. "I forgot about that. Are you sure you're okay to handle it? You know, with everything?"

I'm not sure if *everything* refers to the divorce papers or the abandoned baby, but it doesn't matter. I've been waiting weeks for this meeting, and I'm not going to pass it up.

"I'll be fine," I say. "Marco is an old friend. He's doing this as a favor."

"I'm here if you need me," she reminds me, before turning the corner, walking into her pristine, glass-walled office.

Marco is a former co-worker from my newspaper days. He's still working the crime beat, and he's agreed to interview me for an article. The one-year anniversary of Erin's disappearance is coming up, and even though I've accepted the fact she's likely gone forever, I'm hoping getting her name back in the media will bring fresh attention to her case. More than that, I hope it will put pressure on the police to actually do something. It's not like there's some big mystery surrounding what happened to her. We know who erased Erin from this world: Adam.

Looking across the office, my eyes fall on the cubicle that once belonged to her. People have since been hired to fill her position, but they've been given different working spaces; I can't help thinking this is something Viv did for me. A memorial of sorts.

Erin joined the company as part of the marketing team. She always had a bubbly, uplifting personality and was able to easily transition that into the workplace. She launched a ton of different media campaigns, recruiting more business through the company's social media channels.

It's one of the many reasons I believe my sister is dead. How can a person who used to post on social media five or six times a day just disappear? No messages. No contact. No logins. Her credit cards haven't been used. Zero confirmed sightings of her in close to a year.

"Earth to Emily." Steven swats a folded-up newspaper against my desk. "You're looking tired."

Annoyance briefly overtakes my grief. "Haven't you been told it's rude to say that to a person? It's right up there with asking about their age or weight."

"No offense," he says, his hands going up in a surrender. Steven's hair is stiff with gel; a rash of adult acne covers his chin. "I was hoping after lunch we could talk about the campaign for the Denver office."

I stand, grateful for a ready excuse. "Actually, I have a meeting this afternoon. We'll have to pick another time."

I don't tell him that the meeting involves a personal matter. I rarely talk about my private life with people at the office. In return, they don't ask many questions. Everyone here knows about what happened with Erin, and for that reason, most of them avoid me like the plague.

There are, however, a few irritating exceptions. Like Steven.

"Get some sleep, if you can," he says, completely ignoring my earlier lecture. He walks across the room and sits at the desk beside Erin's empty cubicle. Perhaps that's the real reason I don't like him. Steven took over Erin's responsibilities at the company, and the idea that she's even a little replaceable irks me.

I watch as he types on his computer, not seeming to give me, let alone Erin, a second thought. I can't be angry with the world for moving on. That's what Byron is always telling me. It's easier said than done though, especially when the hole inside my chest widens with each passing day, seems to swallow me whole.

My sister is never coming back, but I'm hoping my conversation with Marco will bring Adam closer to justice.

# FOUR

Marco and I meet for lunch at a café close to the office. We've stayed in touch ever since I left the newspaper where we both worked, and, like most other people I know, he reached out when Erin was first reported missing.

A few weeks ago, when I pitched the possibility of running a one-year anniversary story, he jumped at the chance. Erin's disappearance captured a lot of local media attention in the beginning. She was young and beautiful, the ideal type of victim to plaster on the front pages. However, as the case turned cold, so did the interest in her case. People are only willing to follow a story for so long when it leads to a dead end.

Marco arrives a few minutes after me. He dresses as casually now as he did back when I worked in the cubicle beside his. Jeans and a chunky sweater, although I notice his hairline is becoming less full. I stand to give him a handshake, but he wraps his arms around me in a hug instead.

"Good to see you," he says. "How's copywriting treating you?"

"Not a lot of change, but that can be a good thing."

My position at Viv's company definitely pays well, but it's

predictable. I can almost guess what projects I'll be working on depending on where we are in the sales quarter. And if I forget, I have pesterers like Steven to remind me. When I worked at the paper, I was tackling something new every day. Sometimes personal interest stories, covering the opening of a new small business, or the crime beat.

That last category is what Marco specializes in. There's not a lot of crime in our area, but most of what happens is covered by him.

"Thank you for doing this," I say. "It means so much."

"Of course. People need to keep looking for Erin." I wince, and he must notice. "That is why we're doing this, right?"

"I gave up any hope of finding Erin a long time ago," I answer honestly. "My goal is to bring attention to her case and put pressure on the police to make an arrest."

"You still think it's the boyfriend?" He drops the pen in his hand. "Off the record."

I can't publicly accuse Adam of murder; there would be legal ramifications in doing that, but I trust Marco enough to speak openly. He can present the facts of her disappearance and allow readers to draw their own conclusions.

"He was the last person seen with her," I say. "And they had a complicated history."

"How so?"

"Lots of fighting. Things I would consider controlling behavior." I pause. "Adam was a heavy drinker, and that contributed to a lot of issues. She stuck around to try and help him, but you know how that goes."

Marco nods, making notes. "They broke up before she went missing?"

I shake my head. The memory of him appearing at the restaurant, standing over our table, returns. My chest aches with regret.

"Erin and I were close our entire lives. Hell, even as adults we spent almost every weekend together," I continue. "In the months leading up to her disappearance, I couldn't help feeling she was keeping something from me. I think it was their relationship."

It was in the subtle way she would avert her eyes. The way she would change the subject anytime Adam's name was mentioned. Instead of spending her weekends with me, as usual, she'd claim to have other plans. Something about her life had shifted, but I didn't press her about it. My guilt digs deeper.

"Tell me about what the boyfriend's doing now," Marco says.

"Last I heard he was working at that old consignment shop on Fifth," I say, even though I know he works there. I saw him there last week. "There's not much to him. He claims to be in recovery, but I think that's only to keep the police off his back. It's easier for him to blame his poor behavior on the disease."

"Does he have a violent history? Anything I could mention in the article?"

"He had a domestic violence charge from about ten years ago," I say. "Erin didn't tell me about it until they'd already been together for a while. According to him, it was a big misunderstanding."

"Isn't it always?" Marco says skeptically.

"That's what frightens me. I mean, I didn't see it at the time, but looking back Adam is a clear-cut abuser. He has the violent history. The controlling tendencies. The overall failure to launch. And I believe all of that started to weigh on my sister long before she went missing."

"Walk me through what happened that night," he says, picking up the pen again. "As best you can."

It isn't difficult to revisit the details. The last time I saw Erin plays in my mind as I convey all the details of our final meeting at the restaurant.

"I should have stayed," I say to Marco, pulling my focus back to the present. "I shouldn't have left her with him."

"Don't blame yourself."

"I don't," I say, my tone harsher than I'd intended. "I blame Adam. A nearby street camera caught her walking in the direction of a parking garage. Another camera down the street caught his vehicle leaving a few minutes later, but it was impossible to see whether or not Erin was with him.

"After I reported her missing, the police questioned him. He told them after he left the restaurant he went for a long drive in the countryside before returning home. Alone." I shake my head at his ridiculous excuse of an alibi. "They searched his apartment, but didn't find anything out of the ordinary. Until they got to his car."

Marco looks up. "What did they find there?"

"Blood in the passenger seat," I say. "A small amount, but it did match Erin."

"And that wasn't enough for an arrest?"

"The sample was too small. Any decent defense lawyer would be able to play it off as a papercut or clipped nail. It didn't help he'd had the interior deep cleaned before police interrogated him. The idiot didn't clean the outside of the car, though. There was some evidence found on the exterior, but nothing pertaining directly to Erin. Lots of foliage under the vehicle."

"What do you think happened?" Marco asks, before repeating, "Off the record."

"I think they got into a fight after leaving the restaurant. Or continued an argument they were already having. I think he did something to her on the way home, and took her body out into the woods."

"Don't you think they would have found her by now?"

"I was hoping they would, especially after last winter when

everything melted," I say. "You know as well as I do there are tons of places to get rid of a body if no one is searching."

Marco nods, solemnly. "Are the police still looking into him?"

"They're at a standstill," I say. "Everything points to him. He's the boyfriend. Last person to see her. Their history. He just happened to go on a drive in the country the night she disappeared." I exhale in annoyance. "None of that is enough for an arrest, let alone convincing a jury. Part of me worries we'll never know what happened to her unless he tells us."

"I'm guessing he denies all involvement."

I nod, my expression morphing into one of determination. "But I don't believe him."

"I'm sorry, Emily," he says. "I wish you had more to go on."

"Hell, he's such an idiot, I'm surprised he hasn't confessed to someone by now. I keep hoping he'll fall off the wagon and let something slip." I shudder, suddenly aware of how heartless my comments must come off. "I know that sounds horrible."

Marco shrugs, seemingly unfazed. "If he did confide in someone, a public reminder like this might be what that person needs to come forward."

"Do you think it'll be enough for an article?"

"I have plenty. Besides, you know how the public eats up a good mystery." He taps his hands against his writing pad before his expression changes. "I only wish it wasn't revolving around your sister."

"Me too," I say.

"I can put all the information out there and let people make their own conclusions," he says. "I'll try my best."

"Thank you." I reach my hand across the table and squeeze his. "Also, I wanted to ask. Are you covering the story about the abandoned baby?"

"Yeah, although there's not much to go on," he says. "I

haven't even published an article. How did you hear about it? Still following up with old sources?"

I shake my head. "She was actually left at my house."

Marco's jaw drops. "You're kidding."

"I'm not."

"That's unbelievable," he says. "In the reports I read, the caller's name was redacted. I had no idea. It must have been surreal."

"It was definitely unexpected. And unsettling. Makes you wonder what kind of world we're living in."

Marco taps his notepad again. "When you work the crime beat, you ask yourself that question every day."

# FIVE

I don't return to my car after my conversation with Marco, opting to walk the idyllic streets of downtown instead. Storefronts are adorned with seasonal wreaths, vibrant flags hanging above doors. I remain on the sidewalk, comforted by the warm breeze as I move in the direction of residential neighborhoods.

As I walk, I send Viv a message.

*I'm going to take you up on your offer and go home for the rest of the day.*

Talking about Erin and Adam has exhausted me more than I would have thought. I'm relieved when Viv sends back a quick reply:

*Rest up and take care.*

I'm lucky to have friends like Vivienne and Matt. Even luckier that they're my bosses. I'm not sure how I would have made it through the past year without them.

In the weeks that followed Erin's disappearance, I was a

complete wreck. Each passing day made me agitated, bitter. I was surrounded by well-meaning people—Byron and Viv and Marco—but their presence wasn't enough to make up for my sister's absence.

A month passed without a trace of her. No communication, no phone calls. The police didn't have any leads beyond the evidence they'd found against Adam, but insisted it still wasn't enough. Hope seemed lost.

I quit going to work for a few weeks; anywhere else, I would have been fired, but Viv understood. I started giving up at home, too. Locking myself in the bedroom and refusing to leave for days at a time.

Byron was patient with me, inventing a dozen reasons to coax me out of the house.

*It's perfect weather outside.*

*They're hosting that farmer's market you love this weekend.*

*You can clearly see the constellations in the sky.*

These suggestions only made me angry.

Erin—wherever she was—wasn't enjoying any of these things. The weather and farmer's markets and constellations meant nothing to her. It was then I started to come to terms with the fact that Erin wasn't coming back ever. Erin was dead.

And yet, I didn't get the closure that other families get after a loss. There was no funeral. No memorial. The idea that she was gone yet still out there somewhere was dizzying.

Eventually, I had no choice but to accept my circumstances. I couldn't lock myself inside my room forever. I had to work. I had to keep going. But even when I re-entered society, I wasn't the same person.

It felt like the only contribution I had left for the world was figuring out what happened to Erin. I called the police weekly, and when I wasn't happy with their response, I started calling every other day. The calls were eventually sent to voicemail, my messages never returned.

At home, my marriage wasn't the same either. Byron had taken on more work assignments that sent him out of town, giving me the space I insisted I needed. We began living separate lives under the same roof, the people we were before all but forgotten.

I'm the one who decided to file for divorce. Byron's attempts to help me move on were pointless. I was unwilling to let anyone—even my husband—distract me from uncovering what really happened to Erin. Still am.

My phone begins buzzing inside my pocket. I look down and see that Byron is calling. A year has passed, and he's still trying. It makes me feel guilty. I ignore the call. Hearing his concerned tone isn't something I can deal with right now.

Still following the sidewalk, I cruise past a familiar row of houses, studying each one for subtle changes. Christmas wreaths have been replaced with flower garlands, snowman signs swapped out for wooden Easter bunnies. The world keeps spinning, time marching on, and yet I feel locked in the same place of despair I've been in since the moment I learned Erin was missing; I've just become better at hiding it over time.

My feet stop when I reach my destination, a narrow townhouse that's not as decorative and homey as the others. The gray paint on the siding is worn, as is the red front door, noticeable sun streaks visible from across the street.

I come here when I feel I have nowhere else to go, even though I shouldn't. Even though I've been told not to.

Adam lives here. I like to keep tabs on him, follow him from time to time. There may not be enough evidence to prove it, but I am certain he's the person who murdered my sister, ripped her from the world. I keep thinking, one day, he'll do something to slip up.

I've read about violent criminals, studied the ones that weren't apprehended for their crimes right away. It's common for them to revisit significant places. The location where their victims were killed, or where they disposed of the bodies. More than once, I've followed his car out to the woods, to the area where he claimed to be driving on the night of Erin's disappearance. Breath held, I've watched as he exits the car, only to do something unimportant. Snap a picture or pour out an old drink. Once, I caught him taking a leak on the side of the road. I've never seen him do anything suspicious, like visiting a particular spot over and over again.

Sometimes I wonder if Erin meant so little to him that he has no reason to visit her grave; maybe he's even colder than the violent criminals I've read about.

The front door opens and Adam comes out of the townhouse, as though I've manifested him into existence. He's holding a garbage bag. He descends the cement steps connecting the house to the sidewalk, depositing the bag in the large trash bins by his front gate.

Like an animal that knows it's being watched, he raises his head, checking the area around him. I lower my head and duck behind a lamppost, hoping he won't spot me. He's caught me following him before and complained to the police about it.

The ridiculousness of such an accusation! He gets away with murdering my sister but feels violated because I follow him occasionally. Adam hasn't filed a restraining order. Yet. Although he came close once.

After weeks of no leads and no communication from the police, I needed an outlet for my frustrations. I'd never confronted Adam directly. My tactics were aggressive, not threatening. I operated under the belief that if I kept pushing his buttons, one day his tightly wound façade would slip, and he'd reveal something. On my lunch break, I parked my car outside the secondhand store where he worked and started pasting flyers on the walls of the building. By the time his shift ended, there were dozens of snapshots of Erin's face staring back at him, and all the other bewildered strangers that passed.

After that incident, the police warned me to stay away from him, but they aren't too forceful about it. They probably feel sorry for me.

Everyone, inevitably, pities me.

Byron was furious with me over the incident. Shouting about how getting the police involved could have negative repercussions for us, especially him, as a journalist. He was afraid if I kept making a spectacle he could lose his job, and then what would he have left?

Byron couldn't understand. Erin wasn't his sister. He couldn't see that without her I'd already lost everything.

After Adam goes back inside, I stay a second longer, trying to think about what Erin's last night must have been like.

Did he bring her back here? Maybe they went straight to the woods. When he attacked her, I wonder if it took her by surprise. Or did she see it coming, and not have the strength or resources to do anything about it?

It kills me that I don't know exactly what happened to her, but I promise someday I will.

It's a short walk back to my car at the diner. From there, I drive home. I have a rare feeling of joy about how I can spend the rest of my day. Order some takeout. Turn off my phone. Binge-watch some mind-numbing television program to take my mind off everything.

Who knows? Maybe I'll get wild and sign the divorce papers.

When I pull into the driveway, I'm surprised to see that there's already a car parked in my regular spot in front of the garage. The hairs on the back of my neck immediately stand at attention. It's not Byron's car, or anyone else's I recognize. Perhaps it's the paranoia of knowing I was just spying on Adam. The last thing I want is someone doing the same thing to me.

Relief takes over when I see the person sitting in the driver's seat. It's Tabitha, the social worker from the other night. When she sees me exiting my car, she does the same, smiling tightly.

"You said you'd be following up," I say. "I thought you meant over the phone."

"I hope you don't mind me stopping by like this," she says. "This might be a better conversation to have in person."

The blood in my veins turns ice-cold. "Is everything all right with the baby?"

"She's fine," Tabitha says, holding out her hands. "Appears to be about five months old. Completely healthy. And quite happy, I might add."

"Good," I say.

"Do you mind if we go inside?" Tabitha asks.

I'd hoped whatever follow-up questions she had for me would be brief, and I'm annoyed that her visit will interfere with my plans of lazy television-watching.

I unlock the front door, unload my belongings at the coatrack in the foyer and invite her inside.

"Can I get you anything to drink?" I ask.

"I'm fine," she says, sitting upright on the couch. I notice she no longer appears as easygoing as she did before. There's a strange aura around her, as though she's here against her will.

"What's going on?" I ask her.

She clears her throat. "I wanted to follow up with you. Like I said, the baby was examined at a hospital. She's completely healthy. Really easy, too. All she needs is a warm bottle and she goes right to sleep. It's been a relief, actually. Seeing a child who seems at peace despite their circumstances."

"I'm happy to hear that," I say, still perplexed about why Tabitha looks so disturbed, especially after delivering good news. "What do you need from me?"

"When I came here the other night, I thought you looked familiar," she says. "Your sister is Erin March. The woman who went missing last year."

I clear my throat. "Yes."

"I remember seeing you on television. I followed the case at first, but it fell off my radar after a while." She pauses. "They never found her?"

"No." I look down, clenching my hands into fists. "If I'm being honest, I don't think she's with us anymore. After all this time, we're just looking for a body."

Tabitha nods and exhales, reaching into her satchel. "You remember the saliva sample we collected from you? We run that against the child's DNA, just to ensure it's not some type of unreported home birth."

"Right."

"The problem is, there was a match." She pauses. Her voice is shaking. "Between you and the baby."

My entire body goes hot. "What?"

"Not a maternal link, but you are related to the child left on your doorstep." She pauses. "Do you have any other family in the area? Anyone in their childbearing years?"

"Only my mother," I say. "We rarely talk, but I'd know if she had a baby. Actually, it's not possible. She had a hysterectomy years ago." I pause, trying to gather my thoughts. "What are you saying?"

"You are biologically related to the child left on your doorstep," she repeats, her tone formal, making sure I understand exactly what she's telling me. "You're not the mother, which leads us to believe your sister might be."

My head feels like it's stuck in a hurricane, thoughts and information swarming around too fast. "You think Erin is alive? You think she had a baby?"

"I don't know for sure," she says. "All that's clear is that the child is related to you. You're the next of kin."

# SIX

It feels as though I'm falling. Everything around me appears swirled and misshapen. The floral wallpaper, the dangling glass light fixture, the stone face of the fireplace. The dancing images bend and shake; I fear I might lose consciousness.

Tabitha's voice brings me back to reality.

"Do you understand what I'm telling you?" she asks, clearly concerned by my reaction.

I stand, my balance wavering, as though I'm still locked inside the funhouse maze around me. I stumble into the kitchen and fill a glass with water. It's not until the liquid hits my throat that the world normalizes.

"No," I say, my throat hurting. "I don't understand what you're saying at all."

Tabitha stands and joins me in the kitchen, her hands clasped in front of her body. "I imagine it's quite the shock. I almost didn't believe it myself when I saw the results." She hesitates. "I insisted I break the news to you first. Give you time to adjust to the situation. The police will want to talk to you more in-depth eventually."

"Situation," I repeat the word. It doesn't seem fitting for the reality in front of me. The baby on my doorstep is related to me. Through Erin. There must be some kind of mistake. "You're saying Erin could be alive?"

"Your sister's remains were never recovered."

I turn to face her. "She hasn't been seen by anyone in over a year. Hasn't left a digital trace either. She was last seen with her boyfriend, Adam, an alcoholic abuser with a violent record. His alibi is weak." I pause, out of breath from revealing so much information at once. "There's never been any reason to think she's still alive."

"Until now," Tabitha says, stepping closer. Her demeanor softens to something almost maternal. "This should give you hope."

"But it doesn't make any sense. If she's alive, why hasn't she contacted me? Contacted anyone? And you're telling me she had a baby sometime during the year she's been missing."

"There might be other circumstances we're not aware of. She could have walked away from her life and is now having second thoughts. She could be being held against her will."

"Erin would never have walked away from me," I say, rejecting that theory immediately, a familiar annoyance rearing its head. "And if she's being held against her will, how did the baby get here?"

Tabitha shakes her head and shrugs. "I don't know. I'm the first to admit there's not a lot that makes sense here, but the DNA results are concrete."

The image of the baby returns. Her presence was so shocking, so unexpected, and then fear took over. Any hope I had of understanding the reason for her appearance was replaced with concern over her safety.

This woman is telling me that child belongs to Erin. That wiggling little infant is my niece.

"I... I don't know what to say." As delighted as I am that Erin could be alive, I'm equally overwhelmed by the impossibility of this situation. The joy inside my chest is surrounded with fear and uncertainty; nothing could be more devastating than having this hope that she's still alive ripped away all over again.

"I can't imagine how you're feeling," Tabitha says, as though she's somehow peered inside me and witnessed my whirlwind of emotions. "I want to give you time to process, but you will have to start making some decisions."

"Decisions?"

"Usually, in a situation like this, the child goes into foster care. That is, unless there's a next of kin involved."

"Okay, so now what?"

"The baby can still go into the system, unless you want to take temporary custody."

"What, like take care of her on my own?"

Never in my adult life have I felt capable of having a child; it's one of the other problems that arose in my marriage. Even if I'd acquiesced to Byron's desires and gotten pregnant, I would have been given nine months to prepare, time to wrap my thoughts around the enormity of the change taking place. The suddenness of being asked to take custody of the baby left on my doorstep makes me feel dizzy.

And yet, it isn't just any child, as I'd thought when I first heard her cries. This is Erin's baby. My niece. I recall the feel of her pudgy body in my arms, the ache of sadness when I couldn't soothe her. Why couldn't I have sensed it then? That this baby was a part of my sister, a part of me.

"Our first priority is always to reunite families. If you aren't willing to take custody, the child will be placed in the system."

My knees wobble, the room starting to swim again. I'm not in a position to process any of this. The news that Erin is still alive. That she has a child. That it's up to me to take custody or her baby gets thrown into foster care.

Tabitha sees my conflict.

"You mentioned your mother is in the area," she says. "If you're not willing to take custody, we could contact her."

"No," I say immediately. The child would have better odds being placed with a good family than being given to her.

"These things move quickly. Once the baby is released from the hospital, we'll have to place her somewhere, and if it's going to be in foster care, we'll have to start making arrangements."

"You're telling me I have to decide right now?"

"I know it's overwhelming."

I drink more water, trying to calm myself. This is an enormous choice to make, but the idea of sending that baby to a household of strangers seems impossible.

Of course, I'm a stranger, too.

I think of the baby again, can almost feel the weight of her in my arms. And yet, I only had a few brief moments with her before the officers and paramedics arrived. No, the child I'm picturing is Erin. My adorable, vulnerable little sister. Even as a child, I knew it was my responsibility to protect her, and that's what I did. It's what I continue to do.

Now, it's her child who needs protection, and I'm the only person capable of giving her what she needs.

"I'll do it," I say, quickly. There's no denying I'm unprepared to be a parent, but I'm willing to do whatever it takes to make sure Erin's daughter is safe. "Just tell me what I need to do."

Tabitha reaches into her notebook and tears out a piece of paper. "I'm well aware how sudden this is. This is a list of materials you'd need just to get started. Mandatory equipment. Diapers. Formula. The state may be able to reimburse you for some of these purchases at a later date."

I read down the list, some of the items and brand names so foreign, I wonder, not for this first time, if this isn't some kind of joke, but it can't be. No one would make light of a child's future this way.

"We'd work together to get you approved as the designated guardian. There's a lot of legal hurdles, but I'd be helping you," Tabitha continues. "Are you married? Or would you be raising this child with a partner?"

"I'm in the middle of a separation." My chest clenches. In all the times I'd weighed the possibility of parenthood, I'd never imagined doing it by myself. I can't help wondering if I'm up to the challenge. Especially now that I'm alone.

"I know this is a lot to take on, but my job is to support you every step of the way," she says.

I'm terrified, but I won't turn my back on Erin's baby. We share the same blood, the same history. And yet, there's already so much mystery surrounding her arrival.

How did my niece end up on my doorstep? Is Adam the father?

And, most importantly, what happened to Erin?

# SEVEN

## ERIN

I'm a hopeless romantic. Always have been.

I blame the soap operas. Mom didn't work very hard to give us a happy childhood, but some of the few fond memories I have are late afternoons glued to the television together, watching the latest drama on *Days of Our Lives* and *Secrets*.

For years, I was too young to understand most of the plot lines, and yet I appreciated them in my own way. The love and passion and ambition. Betrayal. Mom would sit in front of the screen, gripped by whatever story was unfolding that week. I'd watch alongside her, waiting for Emily to get home from school.

Emily never liked those shows. She would rather spend hours reading books, sometimes even writing her own stories. She said soap operas were corny and predictable, but that's what I liked about them. The predictability of all the drama being resolved by the end of the hour.

As I got older, and understood more of the emotions at play, I imagined myself as one of the leading characters. My father had taken off before I was even born, and Mom never really dated. The only sense of romance I ever got was from those fictional characters, and whatever boys Emily would date for a few weeks at a time when she was in high school.

Not the most accurate of depictions, sure. But passionate, entertaining? Definitely.

That's why I've never been good with breakups, and this one with Adam is proving especially awful. It's heartbreaking when you think about it, how a person that once made you laugh and smile can turn on you.

It started with the way he'd question me about where I was going and who I was seeing. I felt myself starting to make excuses, coming up with things to tell him so he wouldn't get upset. It created all these barriers between us. Nothing like the love stories I used to watch as a kid.

Adam's behavior always worsened when he was drinking. It's like there were two versions of him. The man drinking liquor was controlling and insecure, but the other him, the real one, was caring and loyal and thoughtful. I fell in love with that version of him; he was my best friend.

"You can't keep living like this," Emily tells me one day. We're at some holiday party, standing in a crowded room with dozens of other festively dressed people. "Give it some time, and you'll see how much happier you are."

Emily is always right, even about this, I suspect. And yet, part of me wants her to be wrong. I want Adam to rush into the room, flowers in his hands, and apologize for his crappy behavior. I want him to say that he's willing to change for me. I want him to dip me for a kiss in a room full of people, like we're the stars of our very own love story.

None of that is real, and yet, wouldn't it be nice if it was?

After the party, Emily offers a ride. She worries I won't get home safely on my own. She has been worrying about me my entire life, it seems. I promise her I'll be fine, that I'm going straight back to my apartment.

That's a lie. The last thing I want to do is spend another night alone with my roommate Beth, especially when all I can do is think about Adam. It's been months since the breakup, but I still find myself thinking about him before I fall asleep, wondering if he's really better off without me, wondering if I'm really better off without him.

Instead of going home, I walk past my complex, decide to have a lonely nightcap at the nearby tavern. We used to come here all the time, Adam and me, before I realized his drinking was the reason for all our issues. It feels different sitting here alone. Strange. Everything feels weird since the breakup. I'm afraid I'll have to learn how to live my life on my own and it's exhausting. Life would be so much easier if we could figure out our problems. Together.

A montage of romantic partners flashes through my mind. I've found myself in a few precarious situations over the years, never having the best judgement when it comes to the men in my life. Emily recounts my ex-boyfriends and thinks I'm dramatic, foolish, but she's wrong.

I strive to see the best in people. We're all human, lugging around baggage and flaws and wounds. Sometimes we must lean on each other to become the best versions of ourselves. Emily has always been that person for me, but deep down, I think I've always desired to be that person for someone else. I desire to be wanted, needed. It's never been my intention to fix the broken men in my life, but when I see another vulnerable person hurting, it's not in my nature to walk away.

And then I see him. He's leaning against the wall. I smile when I recognize him, give a little wave. Across the room, his eyes lock on mine. His gaze makes me blush in a way it never has before.

He comes over, casual at first, and makes some joke. He's always been good at making me laugh, but tonight feels different, as though his words, his presence, are reaching into me, fixing whatever's broken.

"Would it be okay if I got you another drink?" he asks.

I should say no. And yet, something about the way he asks my permission makes me swoon. He's in control. I'm not used to seeing him like this, and it feels like a brand-new version of him is forming before my eyes.

Maybe this is the beginning of another love story, one that's fresh and mature and passionate, just like all those relationships I used to watch as a kid.

I watch as he stands at the bar, waiting to put in our order. He sees me and winks, that one action setting off fireworks throughout my body.

Something is building inside me, a kind of mystical opportunity.

It feels like hope, love.

It feels like a second chance.

# EIGHT

## EMILY

I'm in Walmart, standing in the middle of the infant care aisle.

I've never been more intimidated in my life.

Not even compared to when Mom told me she was pregnant. It was the same conversation in which she told me our father had decided to leave for good. While she was crying and panicking, going on and on about how awful our circumstances were, all I could see was the excitement of having a sibling. Erin. Her presence made up for everything, even my father's abandonment.

Not even compared to when I went to college, several hours away from where I grew up. The campus appeared twice the size of the small town where we lived. Everyone around me already seemed to have friends or connections or money, something weaving them into the fabric of campus life. I was an underprepared outsider, but I was hungry to learn. Better yet, I lucked out by having an excellent roommate. Vivienne. She swooped in and took care of me, like I looked after Erin back home.

In fact, the only bittersweet part of that entire experience was leaving my sister behind. Mom's mental health had deteriorated, and her drinking had worsened, and I worried what leaving Erin alone with our mother would do to her.

I didn't even get butterflies when I married Byron. It was the easiest decision I'd ever made. Byron was my best friend, calm, stable. We met while interning at a local news outlet after graduation. His appearance in my life felt right.

This situation is completely different. A baby.

When I was seven years old, having a baby sister seemed like an adventure. As an adult, I know all the responsibilities that go along with it. I think, with a shudder, I'm starting to sound as hysterical as my mother.

Not to mention, this is undeniably the hardest time of my life. My world has been a mess since Erin's disappearance, and I have no one else to lean on. No sister. No Byron. I'm lucky that Vivienne is still there for me, but I can't really expect her to help. She knows even less about children than I do.

Searching for a distraction, I pull out my phone and search my recent messages, hoping I've missed something. I've called the police station three times since Tabitha left, twice from my living room and once from the parking lot. I've asked to be connected to Detective Carson, the person in charge of my sister's case. Each time I've left a message, but still haven't received a response. This shouldn't surprise me. My name must have been logged on the Do Not Answer list by the police ages ago.

I consider calling a fourth time, but realize that would only stall me from meeting Tabitha in time. I shove my phone into my back pocket, defeated.

"Help you find anything?" A worker in a bright-blue vest approaches me. She gives me a cautious stare, like she worries I'm on the verge of shoplifting.

"Just looking," I say, my eyes scanning the racks of supplies.

"First baby?"

"Yeah," I say, following my response with nervous laughter.

"It can be scary at first," she says, then looks at my stomach. "Good thing you still have a while to go. You're not even showing."

I find myself touching my stomach, envisioning the empty space inside it. Having a child is something that's meant to be celebrated, but not when the circumstances are as dire as these. Before Erin went missing, I'd had brief fantasies of what motherhood might look like. I imagined the joyous expression on Byron's face when I told him I was pregnant, a toddler ambling around a front yard lined with a white picket fence. These visions originate from a different lifetime, it seems, one so at odds with the sudden reality I'm facing. Will I ever be able to give this child what it truly needs?

I shake my head, reach into my purse and find the list of items Tabitha gave me.

"Do you think you could help me find this stuff?"

"Sure," the woman says, scanning the list. "Of course, you don't need all this right away."

The situation is too complicated to share with a stranger. I don't even know how I'm supposed to let the people closest to me know that I'm now responsible for a five-month-old baby girl.

"I'd just feel better having everything ready to go," I say.

The woman nods. "I understand. Happy to help."

We spend the next half hour walking up and down the same few aisles, grabbing everything I might need. Diapers, formula, bottles (two kinds in case the child has a preference), multiple pacifiers, burp cloths, sleeping gowns, one of those sucking mechanisms in the shape of a miniature hot air balloon.

"I know this isn't on the list, but it's best to get now," the woman says, picking a tube of diaper rash cream off the shelf. "Trust me, you'll want this on hand once baby arrives."

"Thank you," I say, looking the woman up and down. She

can't be much older than me. "How many children do you have?"

"Three. My youngest just got out of diapers."

"Well, you certainly know what you're talking about," I say. "I don't know how I would have done this without you."

The woman pauses before speaking again. "Do you have someone at home to help?"

"Yes," I say, thinking of Tabitha's promise to guide me every step of the way, but the answer doesn't sound genuine. Tabitha is only there in a professional capacity. My decision to take in this baby means I'll be raising her by myself.

The woman must sense my hesitation, that there's more to the story I'm not willing to share.

"It's tough raising kids on your own," she says. "I was a single mother with my first baby, before I met my husband. My advice? Get a good team of people around you. We aren't built to do this sort of thing alone."

I nod and thank her again, walking on shaking legs to the checkout counter.

I ring up the items and store them away in bags. My income from working at Vivienne's company is pretty good, but even I winced when I saw the price tag. I never would have imagined the simplest amount of items for the tiniest humans on earth would cost so much money.

When I finish loading my purchases into my car, I sit behind the wheel and call the police station. Again. This time, I demand my call be routed to Detective Carson's voicemail, hoping he'll finally understand the urgency of the situation.

I check the time. Tabitha is due to be back at my house within the hour. And she won't be alone. She'll be bringing the baby with her.

The thought of being alone with the baby makes me feel as though I might be sick. Instead of being like my mother, thinking of all the negative implications associated with caring for a child, I need to consider the positives. This isn't just any child. She's my niece. Part of Erin. Part of me.

Losing my sister over this past year has almost ruined everything. I still don't know where she is, what happened to her or why she's been gone so long, but she has a daughter now, and it's my responsibility to take care of her. I'm going to make the most of this situation, regardless of how ill-prepared I feel. In some ways, it's like I'm getting a small piece of my sister back. *Get a good team of people around you*, the store associate said. It would certainly be easier if I didn't have to carry this burden by myself.

I pick up my phone, contemplating who I can call. Announcing I've decided to take legal guardianship of the child that was left on my front porch seems monumental. Even bigger, explaining that that child is Erin's.

Vivienne is the first person to come to mind, but she's likely still at the office. There's only one other person I feel could help me sort through something this huge. Byron.

# NINE

Maybe it's cruel to ask Byron for assistance. After all, the fact I no longer wanted children of my own was a major part of my decision to file for divorce.

Before Erin went missing, we'd talked about having a small family. We'd imagined two children with a close age gap; one or two years apart seemed ideal if we wanted to raise children in a tight-knit environment. Byron and his brother were only two years apart and remained the best of friends until his brother accepted a job out of state. I always resented that Erin was so much younger than me, even though that never weakened the bond between us.

I'd stopped taking my birth control pills the winter before Erin vanished. We weren't officially trying, but there was no longer anything preventing a pregnancy from happening either. I enjoyed the spontaneity of it, knowing that every intimate moment between us could result in a new life, but I wasn't tracking my cycle and ovulation yet. We were just having fun, waiting to see what life threw at us.

The curveball that none of us were expecting was Erin's disappearance. In my heart and mind, her death.

Byron and I weren't intimate for several weeks after that. As he slowly tried to coax me out of my shell, urged me to start enjoying life again, I'd brush him off. When he finally found the courage to ask me about trying to get pregnant again, I told him I needed more time.

And then he found my newly prescribed birth control pills. I should have known better, hid them in a better place. It wasn't typical for Byron to go looking through cabinets. In the months following Erin's disappearance, my housekeeping skills had fallen by the wayside. He was aiming to surprise me with a clean master bathroom when he found them underneath the sink.

"I didn't know you were taking these," he said, holding up the pills as he walked into the bedroom. I sat on the bed, so ashamed by the discovery, I wanted to pull the covers over my head and disappear.

"It's the same prescription I've always used," I said, playing dumb, trying to dodge the truth.

"These look new. Like you just started taking them." He looked at me. "Did you?"

Part of me wanted to lie. I've always been an honest person, but after everything that had unfolded with Erin that changed. It was easier to tell people what they wanted to hear, to avoid expressing my real emotions at all costs.

When I saw the look on Byron's face, how his every happiness seemed to hinge on my answer, I had to tell the truth.

"I started them two months ago."

"Why didn't you tell me?" He sounded hurt. "I mean, I know we haven't been actively trying, but we will again. One day. Right?"

"Having a baby isn't in the cards for me right now," I said.

"Right now?" There was a pregnant pause. "Or ever?"

I could never get why he didn't understand the changes that took place in me after Erin disappeared. He mourned his brother moving away for a new job; imagine what it was like to not know what happened to my sibling at all, to never get the chance to say goodbye.

Erin's disappearance did more than devastate me; it changed the way I looked at the world. It was the first time true darkness, true evil had touched me. Suddenly, the idea of going on with my life as intended—my happy marriage to Byron and the two children we'd dreamed of—seemed impossible. How could I bring two innocent souls into this world? This same world that had stolen my sister from me?

"I don't know if I'll ever be able to have a child," I told him. "It's been too hard losing Erin. I can't imagine—"

"Not everything is ruined because of what happened to Erin," he said, pleading. "Maybe this is what you need. What we need. We can start over."

Starting over meant no longer caring about what happened to my sister, and she was my biggest priority. More important than my husband, who used every opportunity to travel for work and get away from me, more important than the imaginary children I no longer wanted to have.

Asking Byron to stay by my side in the wake of my new take on parenthood felt like too much. I knew Byron wanted to be a father more than anything, and I didn't want to rob him of that.

Now here I am on the phone, explaining everything about the baby. Asking for his help.

When I return home, he's already sitting on the front porch, wearing a smile from ear to ear.

"You could have let yourself in," I say, unlocking the door.

"I know, but I wanted to wait," he says. Even now, amid a separation, he respects my boundaries. "I'm just happy you called."

Again, I feel guilt nagging. I'm dangling what he wants more than anything right in front of his face, but I need someone's help. I can't do this alone.

"Tabitha should be here any minute," I say. "She's the social worker who is handling the case."

"Has she given you anymore information? Any medical history?"

"They don't know anything," I say. "The only reason they know there's a familial connection is because they swabbed me for DNA."

"I can't believe this," he says. "I mean, all this time we thought Erin was dead. She was out there. She had a baby."

"She could still be dead," I say, grimly.

"Clearly she was alive five months ago."

Theories have been circling around the periphery of my thoughts for hours, ever since my conversation with Tabitha, but I haven't allowed myself to fully think them. Saying such things out loud brings them into existence, and a shiver runs through me. Who knows if my sister is alive? And if she is, there's no telling what horrors she's endured in the last year.

"She could have been kidnapped and held prisoner. Forced to have the baby against her will. Hell, she could have been killed the moment she gave birth."

Byron comes over and puts his hands on my shoulders. "You're working yourself up. There's still hope. Erin could have been the one who left the baby here. Who else would know where you live?"

"Adam knows." I can't shake the idea that he's involved. It's the only theory that's made sense in the past year. "Besides, why would Erin bring the baby and leave?"

Byron opens his mouth and closes it. Whatever positivity he's been aiming for is running out. He steps closer, dropping his hands to his sides.

"I don't know what happened to Erin or how any of it relates to what's happening now," he says. "But I promise you, we're going to find out."

For maybe the first time all day, I have a glimmer of hope.

Investigating is in our blood. It's what attracted us both to our careers, and even though I left the reporting world a long time ago, those passions remain. More than ever, when it comes to finding out what happened to Erin.

Someone knocks against the front door. My mind immediately returns to the other night when those mysterious knocks frightened me. Could that really have been Erin at the door, leaving her child behind? Or was it her captor, abandoning Erin's offspring because she is gone forever?

"Are you ready?" Byron asks me, his voice bringing me back to the present. That same baby is on the other side of the door again, but this time there are more plans in place. I nod.

Tabitha stands on the porch, the carrier resting by her feet. She puts a finger to her mouth.

"The baby is sleeping," she says.

Carefully, she picks up the carrier and enters the house. She finds a cozy spot away from windows in the living room and puts the baby down. When she turns, she looks from me to Byron.

"He's here to help," I explain, introducing him. It seems weird to give him any other type of label. Husband. Soon-to-be-ex.

"Were you able to get any of the items on the list?" Tabitha asks me.

"All of them actually," I say. "Although I have a feeling I'm only scratching the surface."

"As I said earlier, you'll have some assistance for that, too," she says, walking over to the table in the dining room. She starts pulling folders out of her bag, explaining more of the legal proceedings involved with fostering.

There's more to do than I ever would have imagined. Official forms that need to be filled out. I'll have to submit to a background check. She's explaining what the next few months will be like when a gulpy cry rings out in the other room.

Byron raises his head, his eyes gleaming with excitement. "Should I get her?"

"Sure," I say. Even though she's here and I've bought hundreds of dollars' worth of supplies and Tabitha has walked me through the legalities involved, none of it seems real.

Byron appears in the dining room again moments later. The baby is wrapped in a blanket, cradled in his arms. He walks slowly, each step as tentative as though he is about to step on thin ice.

"She's beautiful," Byron says.

"She is," I say, looking at her. I hadn't really paid attention before. I was so shocked by her arrival, worried that she was in danger, that I didn't take in any of the details. Her eyes are a deep blue, the same color as Erin's. Her hair is dark and curly, reminding me of my own baby pictures. How didn't I notice any of this before?

"What should we call her?" Byron asks Tabitha. Yet another question I didn't think to ask.

"Whatever you'd like," Tabitha says. "Until we're able to get more information, there's nothing official on file."

Byron shifts his weight from left to right, the movement pleasing the baby. She wears a gummy smile. He stares at her a moment longer before looking at me. "I'm hogging her. Here, take a turn."

I raise my arms and Byron rolls her into my grasp. I expect her to be heavier. The lightness of her weight is almost more frightening. She's so fragile, like glass.

I try mimicking the same motion Byron did. The baby looks at me and bursts into tears.

"It's okay, it's okay," I soothe her, but it has the opposite effect. She just cries harder.

"She could be getting hungry," Tabitha says, stepping closer. "Let me show you how to prepare a bottle."

We follow her into the kitchen, but the baby's wails are too distracting. Thankfully Byron watches Tabitha's every move. When she's finished, she hands the complete bottle to him.

"I can feed her while the two of you finish talking," he says.

"Are you sure?" I ask, although I've already started handing the baby over.

"Not a problem," he says, not even flinching as he takes the wriggling child into his arms. The moment she wraps her mouth around the bottle, her cries stop. Her eyes close, a peaceful look of contentment on her face. My own chest fills with warmth at the sight of her.

She remains silent for the rest of Tabitha's visit. Byron keeps her in the living room so I can continue learning about all the legal jump ropes. By the time she leaves, the baby is asleep, still comforted in Byron's warm arms.

I watch him sit in the recliner, rocking back and forth.

I'm happy the baby's presence has brought him a little bit of happiness, even if it's only temporary. And I'm happy I won't have to tackle my first night with the baby on my own.

I'm going to need all the rest I can get. First thing tomorrow, I'm starting my investigation to find out what really happened to Erin.

# TEN

A loud thumping wakes me.

I'm lying on the living room sofa, the backs of my eyes stinging with exhaustion. I want to move, but when I try to turn, I remain still, my mind and limbs refusing to cooperate with one another.

Another bang.

Could it be the baby again? I must have gotten up at least a dozen times in the middle of the night. She startled every twenty minutes, it seemed. I tried my best to soothe her back to sleep, but the relief was only temporary. Thankfully, Byron was here, helping me whenever my legs were too heavy to stand.

Another sound. This time, it's recognizable. Someone is knocking at the door. I feel as though I've traveled back in time, to the night when the baby was first left on my doorstep.

"Are you going to get that?" Byron asks, his voice the only thing ushering me into wakefulness. I turn my head to see him standing in the kitchen. He's awake, fully dressed. A burp cloth hangs over his shoulder. "There's someone at the front."

I move quickly, as though my speed can make up for lost time, and stumble to the door.

"You look like shit," Viv says. She's holding a covered plastic platter in her hands. Matt is behind her, his face the same shade of embarrassed red as if he'd walked in on me using the toilet. "Did we come at a bad time?"

"No, no," I say, holding the door open wider. "It was a rough night."

"I'd say," she says, stepping inside. Sometime after Tabitha left, while Byron was settling the baby in for a nap, I called to fill her in, explaining the abandoned child on my doorstep wasn't some strange coincidence. She was as shocked as I'd expected, rattling off a dozen different questions. The baby started crying before I could answer them all, and we had to cut the conversation short. The rest of the night is a sleep-deprived blur.

As they walk in, Matt says, "Vivienne insisted we bring lunch."

Lunch? I raise my arm to look at the watch on my wrist. It's noon.

The baby begins crying, the sound reminding me of last night's endless episodes. Nothing seemed to calm her. Even now, I feel like Byron and I are in the trenches of war. How could people willingly go through this? Why would Byron ever think he wanted to have one of these with me?

Then I remember Erin. This is my sister's child. My niece. And because Erin isn't here to protect her, I must take on that role, whether I'm ready for it or not.

"She's a vocal little thing," Viv says, walking through the living room. She stops when she catches sight of Byron in the kitchen. She puts the platter down on the counter.

Byron looks at the baby in his arms, beaming like a proud parent. "She's beautiful, isn't she?"

Viv's cold exterior melts away, swapped for a playful expression. She holds out her hands. "May I?"

Byron walks into the living room, motioning for Viv to join

him on the sofa. They sit beside one another, and he easily slides the child into Viv's arms. Matt stands at the back of the sofa, leaning over to get a better look at her.

"Wow," he says. "She's like a little angel."

My heart sags at the sight of Viv and Matt fawning over the baby. They don't have any children of their own, but I've always imagined they'd make great parents. She told me once they were trying, before Byron and I even started, but that was ages ago. Once the company became such a success, they shifted their focus to that. Starting a family was an afterthought. Now, as I watch them cuddle and coo at the baby, I wonder if they might give parenting another shot.

"How are you feeling, Byron?" Matt asks, straightening up. His eyes cut over to me. "Looks like it was a long night."

"It wasn't that bad," Byron says.

I'm irritated when I realize he means it. Sure, he was up at every hour, just as I was, but it doesn't seem to have the same wear and tear on him. No bags under his eyes. His clothes are clean. He's conducting friendly small talk while I feel like I'm using every muscle in my body to keep my eyes open.

"You'll have to let us know if you need anything else for the baby."

"I already went shopping," I say, my voice surprisingly defensive. It's glaringly obvious I'm not prepared, but it's still embarrassing how apparent that is to the people around me. Byron is acting like he's part of the household again, all because I can't handle it.

"And don't worry about work," Matt says. "Take off as much time as you need."

"I'm not taking off work," I say, that defensive tone back. "I mean, obviously today I am."

"It's totally normal to take some time when there's a new baby," Viv says. "It's like maternity leave."

"I didn't have a baby," I say, standing so suddenly I start to feel dizzy. "I'll have to go back to work."

"We just don't want you to worry about it," Matt says, his voice more like a question, afraid I'll lambast him for saying the wrong thing. "Really, we want to help."

Byron stands and steps closer, then stops. I believe he's torn between whether he should comfort me or the baby, who is beginning to wiggle in Viv's arms. Likewise, I'm conflicted over him being here. We're on the verge of divorce, but part of me doesn't know how I would have made it through the past twenty-four hours without him.

"Just focus on you and this little one," Viv says, bouncing the baby on her knee. "I don't know how you even wrap your mind around something like this, but you have plenty of time to come up with a plan."

"Plan?"

"Well, when you do come back to the office, you're going to need some type of childcare," she says. "I can ask around for some recommendations."

"All I care about is finding out what happened to Erin," I say, rubbing my palm across my forehead. "Now that we know she had a baby, it puts everything in a different light. I need to revisit everything in her life leading up to her disappearance."

"Okay," Viv says, sitting up straighter. "Where do you start?"

"I don't know," I say, leaning harder into the backrest. "I'll talk to the people in her life. Her old roommate."

There was already a lot of overlap between Erin's circle and mine. Until she got with Adam, she spent most of her time with Byron and me. We worked alongside Viv and Matt. It doesn't seem there could be that much about her life I don't already know, but as my gaze lands on the baby in Viv's lap, I wonder if that's true.

"I know I've asked you this before," I say, leaning forward.

"Did you notice anything strange at work before she went missing?"

Viv and Matt share a look before she turns to me. "Everything seemed normal," she says. "That's why her disappearance never made sense."

In the days after she vanished, this was a popular take. Erin was a young girl, a free spirit. Maybe she'd decided to take off for a few days to figure things out. But I knew my sister. From the moment that first call went to voicemail, I sensed something was wrong.

"Just think about the month before she went missing," I say. "Do you remember anything out of the ordinary?"

"She asked for some time off work," Matt says. "I wouldn't necessarily call that strange."

And yet, I don't remember Erin telling me she had plans to travel. If she were going somewhere, or had something to do, I would have known about it.

"Erin always did a great job with her campaigns," Viv says. "You know my mantra at the office. As long as the work gets done, I don't care how anyone does it."

"Did she say what she wanted time off for specifically?" Byron asks.

I'm surprised to hear him speak. It's like he's following the same train of thought as me.

"She didn't." Matt's gaze turns shifty. "I assumed she was spending time with Adam again."

My hands clench into fists. Everything comes back to him. Adam. He ruined her life the moment he entered it. It was clear to me, and any other outsider, but less obvious for Erin. She deemed his control, worry, his obsession, love. It bothers me to think there were things about her relationship with him she kept secret from me.

Viv sits forward, handing the baby back to Byron. He takes her with ease, a total natural when it comes to children.

"I understand why all this is on your mind considering the circumstances," Viv says. "But I don't want you to start obsessing over a case you can't solve. Erin isn't the priority anymore. You need to conserve your energy for the baby."

Just then, the infant lets out a cry, as though she's joining the conversation.

"I think she's getting hungry," Byron says, looking at me. "You think you can grab a bottle?"

I walk into the kitchen, surprised by how messy the space is up close. Clumps of powder dust the countertops, and there are little moons of condensation from where the bottle has been put down and picked up repeatedly. I open the can of formula, trying to remember how many scoops I need for each ounce of water, but my brain feels like complete mush.

Viv comes to stand next to me, putting her hand on my shoulder. "I can help you," she says. "Perks of being in charge means I can take off whenever I want."

"I appreciate that," I say, smiling. "But I'll be okay. Byron's here."

"For how long?" she whispers.

I haven't thought about it. Byron has always been part of my life, until he wasn't. Despite our looming divorce, he dropped everything to be here for me. And the baby.

"Like you said, there's a lot we need to discuss. Plans we need to make," I say. "All I need is a few more days to adjust."

"Take all the time you need," she says, squeezing my hand.

I appreciate her offer. Protecting the baby and finding out what happened to Erin are my only priorities now. The existence of the baby is proof that I must start looking harder for Erin.

"What have you decided to call her?" Matt says.

"Call her?" I say, blanching. Of all the thoughts that have rumbled through my head in the last few hours, this isn't one I'd considered.

"Well, yeah," Viv says. "You can't keep calling her *the baby*."

But giving this child a name feels like over-reaching. Erin should make that decision. Erin should be here with her.

"I don't know," I say. "I guess I'll add that to the list of things to do."

"Don't let this food go to waste," Matt says, heading towards the door.

Byron shifts the baby into one arm so that he can wave goodbye. Viv stands, watching me, like she's not convinced she should leave. "Are you sure you don't want me to stay?"

"You've done enough," I say, shaking the bottle in my hand. "Please, go enjoy your day."

I watch my best friend and her husband leave the house, my life feeling so far removed from the last time they visited our home together. I look at the baby resting in Byron's arms and feel an internal warmth spreading throughout my body. My life revolves around her now, making sure she's loved and cared for and, most importantly, protected.

But in order to keep her safe, I must unravel the mystery behind what brought her here. I must find out what happened to Erin.

# ELEVEN

The baby stops crying as soon as Byron puts the bottle in her mouth. Her little arms flail in excitement, her full-chest breathing beginning to regulate.

"They have a point," Byron says, eyes on the baby. "We'll have to call her something."

"I have no idea what to name her." I make no attempt to hide my annoyance now that we're alone. I've always been my complete self around Byron, which is part of the reason we're getting divorced. For the past year, I've been a miserable person.

"We need to talk about other things, too," he says.

"Like what?"

"As Viv mentioned, you're going to have to start thinking about childcare. How you're going to fit this baby into your life. I took off the rest of the week—"

"You did what?"

"Don't worry. I didn't tell anyone anything. And it's not like I won't be working at all, I'm just going to do some work from home." He pauses. "I thought you could use the help."

My relief outweighs my frustration. "You didn't have to do that."

"I know." He pauses again. "I appreciate you letting me stay overnight. I won't make it a habit."

"That's probably for the best." The familiar hole in my heart returns. The sting of our breakup is still fresh, even if I think it's the right decision for us to be apart.

"Just tell me whatever you need me to do," he says. "I'm not going to feel comfortable leaving until I know you're settled."

I look down at the infant in his arms. Her eyelids flutter closed, small hands pulled close to her chest. I still can't believe that this baby came from Erin, that she's a part of her. Part of me wants to stay by her side always, to protect her, but if I do that, I won't get any closer to finding out what happened to her mother.

"Do you mind staying here with her? I want to go and talk to Beth."

"Do whatever you need to do," he says, smiling.

I look down again at the sleeping baby. "You really are a natural at this."

Byron has always wanted to be a father. Even now, he's jumped at the chance to help. I don't want him to think this is his invitation to start playing house again, but I'm not ready to be alone with the baby. Not yet. I must figure out what happened to Erin first.

"Think you could pick up some more baby wipes while you're out?" He slowly lowers himself to the sofa, careful not to wake the sleeping child. "I think you horribly underestimated how many we'll need."

I laugh. "Sure. Be back when I can."

* * *

There are certain places around town I find myself drawn to over and over again. Adam's apartment. The woods where he goes driving. The restaurant where I saw Erin for the last time.

Likewise, there are places I try to avoid, the memories they evoke too painful.

Erin's apartment is one of them.

I remember moving her in, Byron and I dripping in sweat as we heaved her secondhand sofa up to the third floor. I remember the party she threw once everything was finally sorted. I remember coming over here on Christmas morning before last, after we'd vowed we were done making the trek out to Mom's house just to witness one of her hangovers.

I stand on the sidewalk, staring up at the gray, brick walkup. Each unit has a large patio jutting out from the side, yet another location of countless memories. I force myself to take one more breath before heading to the buzzer.

"Yeah?" a voice answers on the other end. Beth, her roommate.

We were in constant contact in the weeks following Erin's disappearance, but we've since lost touch. Just the sound of her name brings back sad memories about Erin. I wasn't even sure if she still lived here.

"It's Emily," I say. The pause that follows makes me hold my breath.

"Long time no see," Beth says, her voice more animated than when she'd first answered the buzzer, if a little hesitant. "What do you want?"

"There's been some updates with Erin's case," I say. "I wanted to run them by you."

The last time we spoke, our conversation nearly ended in a fight. Beth must be debating whether or not to feed me some excuse as to why we can't meet. Then again, her curiosity over what new developments might exist must be overpowering.

The front door clicks, and I enter, the musky scent of the stairwell surrounding me as I climb to the top floor. Beth is waiting at the apartment's entrance. Her posture is rigid, unsure how to greet me.

"How've you been?" She scans me up and down, as though looking for signs of weakness. Or maybe it's the other way around. Maybe she's threatened by me.

"Okay, considering." I pause. "Is this a bad time?"

"I just finished up lunch," she says, walking back into the apartment and nodding for me to follow. "I'd been expecting you."

"Really?" My eyes bulge in surprise. Considering how things went the last time we spoke, I thought she'd never want to talk to me again.

"The one-year anniversary is coming up," she says, sitting in an armchair by the window, a rather lacking view of downtown behind her.

"Right," I say. Two days ago, it had been the anniversary that was dominating my thoughts. One year without Erin. One year since she died. Now, with the appearance of my niece, everything has changed.

"There's something I need to tell you," I say, sitting across from her, hoping to avoid a stroll down memory lane.

"Oh no." She moves immediately, perched on the edge of her seat, worry clouding her eyes. "Do you have news?"

She thinks I'm here to tell her we've found a body. It's a conversation I've imagined and dreaded a dozen times.

"Nothing like that." I pause, gathering my thoughts. "What I'm about to say isn't in the media yet. I'd like you to keep it between us."

She nods, listening intently.

I take a deep breath. "The other night, someone knocked on my door. When I opened it, there was a baby sitting in a carrier on my porch."

Beth's jaw drops. "You're kidding me. Like, a real baby?"

"I wish I was," I say. "My house is close to a fire station. I thought someone was intending to drop the baby there and chickened out. Turns out, it's more complicated than that."

Her brow furrows in confusion. There's even a mild annoyance in her expression as she wonders how any of this is related to Erin. "What do you mean?"

"The police did some DNA testing." I take another deep breath. "The baby is related to me. Through Erin."

Beth sits back, like she can't quite believe what I'm saying. Her mouth opens and closes several times, as she debates what to say. "Erin has a child?"

"Yes," I say. "A five-month-old."

Beth stands unsteadily and begins to pace. It's bizarre, watching as Beth experiences the same series of emotion and confusion I felt the other night. "Does that mean Erin is alive? Do you think she's the one who left the baby on your doorstep?"

The rapid succession of her questions mirrors my own thoughts, the difficulty of trying to make sense of such a bizarre situation.

"I'm not convinced Erin is the one who left her," I say, giving the answer I've had some time to consider over the past two days. "If she brought the baby, I don't know why she would have left."

Beth stops, turning to face me, her face changing. "I'm so sorry, Emily. This is the last thing you need, after what she's already put you through."

I stand too, sensing a sudden shift in her demeanor. "What are you saying?"

"I mean, this changes everything, doesn't it? This whole time you've been thinking she was dead or abducted—"

"She could still be abducted." It pains me to say it. It's a possibility I don't want to consider, my little sister being chained up in some creep's basement, forced to endure unspeakable abuse day after day, eventually resulting in a child. I don't want to think she could be dead either. That she was discarded the moment the baby was born, no longer needed.

"Right," Beth says, wincing at the thought. "But given the

fact we know she's been alive most of this year now, it could also mean she just left."

There it is. The same accusation Beth made months ago during our last conversation. Initially, Beth was supportive, helping me hang up flyers and updating social media with relevant information pertaining to Erin's case. As the weeks went on, she started to question whether Erin left intentionally. She told me her theory, and I lashed out at her.

I cock my head to the side. "Erin didn't leave on her own."

"I think you have to consider the possibility," she says, hesitantly. "Especially now."

The last time we spoke, she asked me if I'd ever considered the idea Erin simply ran away, left willingly. She pointed out that Erin's suitcase was missing, as were some of her favorite clothes, but that was a weak argument. Erin wasn't a big traveler. There was no way of confirming if or when she'd gotten rid of her suitcase, but it could have been weeks before she went missing. Likewise, the few articles of clothes she mentioned could have easily been misplaced, damaged or donated. There wasn't enough missing from her room to suggest she willingly walked away from her life.

I told Beth all of this, accused her of being selfish, of never being Erin's true friend. She insisted my sister was troubled and I was in denial. She claimed she wanted to move on with her life, something I didn't have the luxury of doing. There is no life for me without Erin.

The memory of that conversation sends a wave of outrage coursing through me.

"Erin had no reason to walk away from her life."

"I'm not trying to upset you again," Beth says, her hands little white flags in front of her body, begging for peace. "If the child is five months old, it's possible she knew she was pregnant before she went missing. Maybe she went away on her own to process."

"Process what?"

"I don't know," she says. "An unplanned pregnancy."

I consider Beth's theory. A young, frightened girl falls pregnant and doesn't know how to cope, so she runs away until she can figure out what to do. It makes sense, if she was talking about some stranger, but not when it's Erin.

"If Erin were pregnant, she would have come to me," I say. "And it doesn't explain anything else. She's not used any of her credit cards. Hasn't contacted anyone. Her blood was found in Adam's car!"

"I remember all of that," Beth says, but her response is unconvincing. "It's just, she was so secretive in the weeks leading up to her disappearance."

"Secretive?" The anger in my voice startles me. I remind myself this is precisely why I came here, to re-investigate what was going on in Erin's life before she went missing. I force myself to listen. "What do you mean?"

"I already told you," she says cautiously, for fear I might lash out at her again. "There were several mornings I woke up and she hadn't come back from the night before."

"She'd rekindled her relationship with Adam and didn't want to tell us," I say, my irritation growing. "You know this."

"That's what you think, I know," Beth says. She bore witness to Adam's controlling behavior as much as I did. When Erin made the decision to get back with him, she would have been disappointing both of us. "But there were other things, too. Like the money problems."

Another point of contention between us. Erin had been missing several weeks when Beth first explained my sister had fallen behind on paying her rent and utilities, something else that was never like her. Erin could be flighty. More than once, I'm sure she saw the need for an extra nightcap instead of putting money away, but it was completely unlike her to quit paying her bills altogether. I chalked it up to another result of

Adam's abuse, a side effect of the stress he was adding to her life. I wrote Beth a check to cover the missing expenses, and that was the end of it.

Or so I thought. Now I wonder if the petty roommate drama is coloring Beth's opinion of my sister's case.

"All I'm saying is, there were things going on with her," she says. "If she knew she was pregnant, maybe that's why."

"If Erin was pregnant, she would have come to me," I repeat.

"But she didn't," Beth says, abruptly. "And really, she wasn't acting much like Erin at all those last few weeks. Things she would have normally told me, or you, she kept secret. I've never wanted to say any of that because she was a victim. Your theory about Adam lines up, and I didn't want to blame the dead.

"But now that we know she was alive, at least five months ago, it makes me wonder if there was a reason she was hiding so much. Maybe she knew she was pregnant and planned on leaving."

The theory infuriates me, and I struggle to keep my composure.

"If she planned on leaving with the baby, why would she bring her back?"

Beth shrugs. "Parenting is hard. Maybe Erin realized she couldn't do it on her own and decided to give up responsibility."

"Erin would not give up her baby."

"If Erin chose to walk away from me and you and the rest of her life," Beth says, "I'm not sure what she would do."

My hands clench into fists. I'm about to say something else, another defense of my sister, when a noise across from the apartment grabs my attention. A door is opening. The door to Erin's bedroom. I haven't been in there for so long. The last time I was here, Beth still had all her belongings, as though Erin never left. I long to see her room as it was, usher in happy memories of when we were here together.

Without thinking, I march in that direction, catching someone just as they exit her room. It's a man. One I recognize. He freezes when he sees me standing in front of him.

"Steven?" I ask, my voice high-pitched with shock. I've only ever seen him at the office, sitting at the desk beside Erin's old cubicle. I can't believe he's walking out of her bedroom.

"Emily," he says, surprised. "What are you doing here?"

"This is Erin's apartment," I say, my irritation growing. "Why are you here?"

"Emily, you can't just start interrogating random people!" Beth shouts.

"He's coming out of Erin's room!" I say, looking back at Steven. "And he's not random. We work together."

"It isn't Erin's apartment anymore," Steven says, plainly. "I started renting out this room from Beth several months ago."

"And you didn't think about mentioning that to me?"

Steven and I barely talk at work, but he, like everyone else at the office, knows about Erin's disappearance. He knows I've believed her to be dead this past year. It's bad enough he replaced her at the company, but it seems eerily convenient that he'd move into her old apartment, too.

"I didn't see the point in telling you. It wouldn't..." he pauses, struggling to find the right word, "help anything."

Embarrassment burns my cheeks. Steven stands at the door awkwardly.

"Care to let me pass so I can get back to the office?" he says, finally.

"Sure," I say, taking a step to the side.

I fight the urge to open the door behind him, to look into the room that once belonged to my sister. The memory remains singed in my brain. Her tufted lilac comforter. Framed concert posters on the wall. Fairy lights hanging in the corners of her windows. It doesn't seem that long ago that I was here, visiting her. I forget a whole year has passed, bringing with it countless changes.

"You never told me you were looking for a new roommate," I say.

"It's not really your business," she says, harshly. Her balance shifts from one foot to the other, and she softens her tone. "I couldn't afford to keep the place without one. Not like it was easy finding a renter either, considering I had to tell them my old roommate was the victim of foul play."

"She could still be the victim of foul play."

"Since Steven worked with her, he already knew the story," she says. "It was a win for both of us."

Her choice of words feels like an arrow in the chest.

"I'm sorry if my reaction was too harsh earlier," she says, moving closer. "But don't you think it at least sounds a little bit like Erin? Finding herself in a difficult situation and convincing herself it's easier to skip town than admit what she did?"

The way she says this bothers me, maybe because it strikes a chord of truth. Erin could be irrational and quick-witted, but she has been gone over a year. There's no way one of her episodes would have lasted that long. She wouldn't do that to me.

"What did you do with Erin's things?" I ask, looking back at her bedroom.

"I boxed everything up—"

"And didn't give them to me?" I cut her off, eager for a reason to be angry.

"You seemed so..." her voice is small, struggling to find the right word, "...intense, the last time we spoke."

As if I didn't have plenty of reasons to be overly emotional. For a year, I've believed my sister was dead. The judgement in Beth's voice slices right through me. She's judging me, judging Erin. My sister isn't perfect, but she deserves to have more people in her corner.

"I should go," I say, needing to escape. I also don't want to say anything that could deepen the divide between Beth and me.

"I wasn't trying to upset you," Beth says, following me.

"You already said that."

The hard truth I must accept is that it will be impossible to start digging into my sister's past without uncovering things that are hurtful. I must grow thicker skin.

"I'll be thinking of you," Beth says, standing in the doorway. "And the baby."

# TWELVE

## ERIN

Three Months Before the Disappearance

I feel alive again.

After the breakup, my life seemed drab and muted. But now? The world seems vibrant and fresh and new. I wake up excited for what's to come, excited to see him.

Of course, we don't get to see each other every day. The times in between are excruciating, like I'm trapped under water waiting for the moment I can finally breathe again. When we're together, everything is easy and fun and meaningful. Different from all the times before.

We meet at our special place, where we don't have to worry about being interrupted. As soon as the door closes behind us, he swoops me into his arms, his lips grazing my mouth and cheek and neck. The passion brewing between us is electrifying. He didn't used to make me feel this way. No one did.

"I don't think there's ever been a time I've been this happy," he says, gasping for breath after we've finished. He pulls up the covers to conceal himself, never once taking his eyes off my bare body. I love the way he looks at me, drinking me in like an addictive elixir. "I love you, Erin."

My chest fills with warmth and excitement. If I could stay in this moment forever, I would.

But I can't, and confronting that reality is difficult. The moments we spend together are such a high, but then he leaves, gone again, and there's nothing there to break my fall. What's worse, I can't tell anyone what I'm going through. Friends at work, Beth, Emily—none of them can know the truth without judging me, so I'm forced to keep everything a secret. For a while, it was fun, but as time passes, it becomes a heavy burden to carry. I realize the more I start to care for him, the more I start to lose pieces of myself.

One morning, it finally hits me. I sit up in bed in a nervous sweat, some horrible nightmare refusing to release me even after I've woken. My heart beats against my ribs, and I raise a hand to my chest, trying to calm myself. At the same time, my stomach clenches, a horrible tension tightening in my head. I run into the bathroom and throw up into the toilet. Afterwards, I splash water from the sink over my face, can barely stand the sight of myself in the mirror.

This isn't a fantasy, a fairy tale, a love story ripped from a television set.

It isn't real, and if I'm going to build the life I want, that's what I need.

How did I get here? It wasn't just one mistake, but a series of poor choices.

I wish there was someone I could turn to who would understand. Normally, I go to Emily with everything, but she won't be able to forgive me for this. I can't imagine confiding in any of my other friends, either. I even consider reaching out to my mother. If anyone understands making difficult choices, it's her. She's always been kinder to me than she has Emily, more forgiving. I decide against reaching out for fear she won't have any real advice to give.

So I'm alone, again. And yet, this time, when I think about that, it isn't so scary. Maybe I'd be better off on my own, away from him and—

Beth bangs on the bathroom door, interrupting my thoughts. "Don't forget rent's due at the end of the week."

"On my calendar," I shout back, even though I don't have a calendar. And I don't have the money for rent right away, either. How am I supposed to better myself when the life I've been living is already in shambles?

I close my eyes and try to imagine a way out of this situation. I wish I were a different person completely, one who wasn't so easily fooled and capable of making mistakes. I wish I could start over, without the reminders of my past weighing me down. I envision a different life for myself in a different place.

When I open my eyes again, I feel lighter. There could be a way out of this after all.

It's time for a change.

# THIRTEEN

## EMILY

I stare at the brake lights in front of me, transfixed by the devilish red glow. I don't notice the lights retreating until the car behind me blares its horn, condemning me for holding up traffic.

The interaction with Beth haunts me. Most of my relationships overlap with Erin, but her friendship with her roommate was all her own. I'd thought Beth would be elated to know there's a possibility Erin is still alive; instead, she floated a different theory, insisting Erin might have left of her own volition, an accusation just as hurtful as the first time she made it.

Sure, Erin could be flighty and unpredictable, but she wasn't the type of woman to up and walk away from her life. Leave her friends and co-workers and family.

She wouldn't leave me.

We've been through too much together.

Our mother was a complicated woman. Even at age seven, I sensed this, and it's why I made such an effort to take care of my baby sister. As the years carried on, we only leaned on one another more. Mom was always there, as consistent and irritating as an HVAC unit forever humming, but we depended on one another for life's big moments. I'd help Erin complete her homework when she was in elementary school; once she was old enough to return the favor, she'd call out study guide questions to me. I still remember the adorable way she'd pronounce words like *trigonometry*.

When she was sick, I'd run to the pharmacy to pick up her medicine, always made sure she had extra spending money for her school field trips. The bond between us was unbreakable, forged through years of neglect and indifference from our mother. Even if Erin decided to leave every other part of her life behind, she would never abandon me.

As I turn onto the four-lane road ahead, a woman pushes a stroller on the sidewalk beside my car, an image that I'd likely never have registered a few days ago. Now I look at this woman, the light-blue hood covering the infant bundled in blankets, and I see myself, Erin, a plethora of mysteries and possibilities.

Did Erin know she was pregnant before she went missing? Is that why she was rekindling her relationship with Adam? Or did she fall pregnant after she left, forced to have a child under unthinkable circumstances? If Erin has been terrorized and tortured since she went missing, that stress could result in a premature labor.

Part of me still can't believe the baby is Erin's at all. I never pictured her as a mother; that's hard to do when, in my mind, she's always been my kid sister. Someone you imagine being forever young, an image that has haunted me in the past year when I thought she was dead.

Another incident comes into my memory. Beth was right about Erin always finding herself in trouble. Adam wasn't her only bad boyfriend over the years. She had a series of reckless flings in high school. I'd get constant phone calls from our mother demanding to know where Erin was whenever she didn't come home or skipped curfew. I figured her teenage rebellion was a result of my mother's issues; I didn't blame her for wanting to be home as little as possible.

Her poor romantic choices followed her to community college. She entered into a relationship with a teacher's assistant. David. I can still remember Erin calling me crying once news of their relationship broke on social media. People called her a slut, called him a pervert. He ended up getting fired for inappropriate behavior, and Erin transferred to a different school. I haven't thought about that in a long time, not since around the time Erin went missing.

While Adam was always the top suspect in my mind, I didn't want to suffer from tunnel vision. I had to consider every other person who could have a reason to do Erin harm. I even looked up David during one of my late-night research binges, trying to see if there was anything that connected him to Erin.

Turns out, he was happily married; his wife had welcomed twin girls three years ago. He certainly didn't seem like the type to hunt down his ex and harm her, even if she did put an embarrassing dent into his teaching career.

Adam was the only person in her life that could have done her harm. I still believe that. I remember the way he looked when he interrupted us at the restaurant. The irritation on his face, as though my presence was impeding something more important.

All this time, I've been convinced he murdered her that night. The baby proves that she didn't die then, but there's still no guarantee she's safe now. Or that Adam isn't responsible.

I pull onto the narrow road leading to my house. When I reach the driveway, my heart aches at the sight of Byron's car. It wasn't that long ago that we were happy, that the idea of being together forever brought me peace. Now, I'm not sure what he means to me, other than a buffer between me and my niece.

Then I notice another car parked on the side of the road, and my stomach drops. It's a dark sedan, like an unmarked police vehicle.

I barely have time to put my own car into park before I'm opening the door, rushing to the porch steps. Another visit from the police can't be good. It never is. What if this is the conversation I've been dreading? What if they've finally found her?

When I walk inside the house, the baby is crying. I hear Byron's voice as he softly shushes her, trying to calm her. Then I hear a second, familiar voice.

The man sitting on my sofa wears a dark suit and has a receding hairline. He stands when he sees me, the badge on his belt gleaming as it catches the light from the window. Detective Carson is the lead investigator on my sister's case.

"Detective Carson?" I say, almost out of breath. "Did you find her—"

"I'm not here about Erin," he says, his voice steady, as though trying to de-escalate my frazzled emotions. "Not exactly."

"He's here about the baby," Byron says, his voice noticeably grim.

"What about her? Is something wrong?"

"Nothing is wrong," Carson says, his voice more assertive. "I received all the messages you left at the station. And your voice-mail. I thought it might be easier to discuss everything in person."

I resent people when they talk to me in that way, with the same tone Beth used. Obviously, everything pertaining to Erin, and now the baby, is going to send off sirens inside me. They should understand that, not judge me for it. Byron cuts his eyes in my direction, but I ignore him; I never told him I'd been pestering the police for fear he'd judge me, too.

"I've been in communication with Tabitha from DCS,"

Detective Carson says once I sit. "She told me you've chosen to take custody of Erin's baby."

"Of course. She's my niece," I say. "I'm hoping this latest development will make you take Erin's case more seriously."

Carson pulls a face, declining to engage. For months, he's insisted he's done everything he can, but that's hard to believe when Adam is still roaming the streets.

"We've established the child's mother," he says. "Now, we need to identify the father. It might give us a lead into where Erin has been all this time."

"We already know who the father is," I say.

"We do?" Carson acts surprised.

"Adam."

His lips form a straight line as he nods. "The two of them have a romantic history and he was the last person seen with her—"

"And her blood was found in his car," I interrupt him, feeling the need to remind him of the details of his own investigation.

He nods again.

"That's why we've asked Adam to take a DNA test," he says. "If we can prove he's the father, it gives us a reason to question him again."

Carson and I have had numerous standoffs in the past year, which has left me defensive. I realize, for the first time, he might actually be here to help.

"I know Adam is the baby's father."

"Until we're able to prove that we can't start answering other questions. How did the baby get here? Where is Erin now?"

My body surges with adrenaline and hope. Finally, we're closer to finding answers.

"What do you need us to do?" Byron says. The baby has finally gone silent in his arms.

"We've already spoken to Adam. He's agreed to meet us at the station tomorrow to do his part. We can run it against a sample of the baby's DNA, with your permission, of course."

The idea of police already contacting Adam only further excites me. "What did he say when you told him about the baby?"

"I can't give you any details," Carson says, his posture stiffening. "That's another reason we'd prefer to collect the sample here. There's no reason to put the two of you in the same room together."

Carson hasn't only been in touch with me about Erin in the past year. He's also the person who warned me to keep my distance after Adam reported me for harassment. It was ridiculous, the idea I could be told who I could and couldn't be around. I hadn't done anything wrong. Adam was the abuser, the killer. Not me.

"I think that's a good idea," Byron says, trying to keep the conversation from spiraling. "Don't you, Emily?"

"Sure," I say.

Carson stands. "I have everything we need in my car. There's some paperwork you'll need to sign."

"Anything we can do to help," Byron says.

Once Carson has left, I look at him, my eyes alight. "Finally. They're going to get proof that Adam is connected to all this."

"Don't get your hopes too high. There's still a lot we don't know." He pauses. "Why didn't you tell me you'd reached out to the police already?"

Because I didn't want him looking at me the way he is now, like I'm a woman unhinged. That old resentment comes back to the fore. Why must Byron always try to temper my emotions, especially when it comes to Erin? I don't understand why he, and everyone else, can't believe what I believe, that Adam is involved.

"It's not a big deal," I say. "I only wanted to make sure the police were re-opening their investigation as soon as possible."

"Did you get the wipes?" Byron asks, looking away, that grating sunshine tone in his voice as he glances at the baby.

"Sorry," I say, frustrated. "Completely forgot."

"Don't worry about it," he says, coming over to me and placing the baby in my arms.

# FOURTEEN

After what seems like an eternity, we put the baby down for a nap. She rests soundly in the pack and play in the living room. I'm cautious to even breathe for fear of waking her.

"What do you think about Rosie?" Byron asks.

"Excuse me?"

"I've been calling the baby Rosie."

My shoulders rise toward my ears. "I think it's weird to name a baby that isn't ours."

"I think it's weirder to keep referring to her as *she* or *baby*," he says. "Besides, technically, she is yours."

This comment startles me. Even though I've taken on guardianship of the baby, I don't look at her as though she's mine. She's Erin's, and right now, the greatest link to the possibility my sister might one day come back.

"I'm only stepping in until we can find out what happened to Erin," I say, defensively. "She should be the one to name her."

"It's not like it's permanent," Byron says, his voice small. "Just something to make the whole situation a little more personal."

I watch the sleeping infant. Rosie. Her eyelids flutter as she breathes, enviable thick lashes curving away from her face. The name suits her, I suppose. It links to her lovely flushed cheeks. I stretch out my fingers and brush them against her face, my touch gentle so as not to wake her.

"How did it go with Beth?" Byron asks.

I sigh. "Not what I was expecting."

"Did you tell her about the baby?"

"Yes, but her reaction surprised me. I thought she'd be like me, excited there was a possibility Erin was alive. Instead, she floated the idea that Erin left on her own."

"Why did she say that?"

I shrug. "She said she thought it seemed like something Erin would do."

The silence between us is heavy. Byron and Erin were always close. She considered him the older brother she never had—not that she needed one when I was around. But there were times he scolded me for being too forgiving when it came to my baby sister, overlooking things about her others wouldn't.

That's what you do when you love a person, I insisted, and I still do. An outsider, even a close one like Byron, could never understand that particular bond I had with my sister. Some of her behaviors might have perplexed others, but I loved her for who she was.

"She had to have a reason for thinking that," he continues, pushing. "Besides the baby."

"She brought up the fact Erin was behind on bills again," I say. Byron nods. He was aware I cut her a check at the time. "I'm not sure why Erin didn't have the money. And if she was short on cash, why would she ask Viv and Matt for time off? There's no telling what Adam got her into."

Byron is silent, thinking. "You still think he's involved?"

"He has to be," I say. "Hopefully the DNA test will confirm what I've always known."

"If Adam is involved, why would he leave the baby with you after all this time?"

It's strange. I've watched him closely for more than a year. If he knew he had a child with Erin, there certainly weren't any warning signs. Never once did I catch him buying diapers or infant toys or formula.

"I don't know. I'm missing something."

Byron stands, walking toward me. "I think what you need more than anything right now is rest. Why don't you take a nap?"

"You've had the baby all day," I say.

"You need sleep, especially if we're going to put in another all-nighter."

I sit up straighter. "We don't need to put in another anything. You've done more than enough already."

"I'm here for you, Em. Always have been."

"You can't be anymore," I say. "That's the point of getting divorced."

I've thought much less about our separation since I learned I was related to the baby, but that dilemma still remains. The paperwork is in this house, somewhere, unsigned. Byron has gone above and beyond to help me, but that doesn't change what we're going through.

"Have you signed your papers?" I ask him.

He shakes his head. "Haven't had time."

I put my hand over his. "Thank you for all the work, but I need to do this on my own. It's something I have to get used to."

He opens his mouth like he wants to say something more but stops. He wears a painful expression, and I shudder in shame at being the cause of his sudden unhappiness.

"All right," he says. "You'll call if you need me?"

I simply nod.

He bends over the pack and play to get a better look at the

sleeping child. He cups his hand and moves his fingers in a little wave. "Bye bye, Rosie."

The happiness as he speaks her name breaks something inside me.

He walks to the front door and grabs his belongings. It looks as though he's leaving for work, something I've seen him do hundreds of times before, but I know now it's different. Permanent. Our relationship to one another will never be the same.

"May I make one more suggestion before I leave?" he asks.

It's the least I can do, considering he dropped everything to be here for me. And the baby. "Shoot."

"I know you don't want to," he says. "But you need to call your mom."

"Are you crazy?" For a moment, I seriously consider whether he's joking. My mother and I don't speak. Ever. "With everything going on, she's the last person I need to deal with."

"She deserves an update, and it would be better coming from you than the police."

He leaves quickly, avoiding my reaction.

# FIFTEEN

The night was horrendous, the rounds of interrupted sleep their own form of torture. Although Rosie is happy to take naps in the pack and play during the day, at night she wants to move. It seemed like neither one of us got a substantial amount of sleep.

The waking hours gave me plenty of time to think about what Byron said about my mother.

We've never been close. Ironically, we've talked more in the past year than we ever have before, and even then, it's only been a handful of times. But Erin is her daughter, this baby is her granddaughter. She deserves to know about what's going on.

I stuff a canvas bag with everything I think I might need. Diapers, bottles, rattlers, wipes—which Byron ended up purchasing and leaving on the front porch sometime before dawn. Getting everything packed and out the door is a headache, only for me to forget my own wallet and keys. I go back inside, triple checking that I have everything I need, and then I begin the short drive to Mom's house.

She lives on the outskirts of town, in the small house we were raised in. As is usual when I make this drive, I'm overcome with memories of Erin, our neglected childhood that somehow felt complete because we had each other. Mom's drinking spiraled out of control once our father left. After everything we experienced growing up, I couldn't understand why Erin would get involved with a drinker like Adam. Maybe she believed she could fix him in a way we never could with our mother.

When I approach the house, I see her black pickup truck in the driveway. She's home, not that I'd expect her to be anywhere else. She stopped waiting tables a few years back, relies on a measly income from the state to get by. I didn't give her any warning about my visit. Some things are just too complicated to explain over the phone.

I lift the baby carrier out of the back seat and walk to the front porch, rapping against the sun-faded wooden door. Footsteps approach from the other side, and I tense with anxiety.

"Emily," Mom says, when she opens the door. "What a surprise."

She has no idea, I think, my eyes darting to the baby carrier.

"Hi, Mom." Despite my resentment, a smile spreads across my face. The sight of her brings back painful memories, but she's still my mother. "We need to talk about Erin."

She trembles, her hand reaching for the doorframe to keep her balance. Like me, she must be expecting the worst news, and I feel a wrinkle of shame that I didn't handle this better.

"They haven't found her," I say, quickly.

Mom wilts in relief. "Thank God."

"There has been a development, though," I say. "One I don't really know how to explain."

I bend down, lifting the carrier at my feet. Mom's eyes widen, her stare bouncing between the baby and me. "Emily, what's going on?"

"Can we come inside?"

Mom watches the carrier suspiciously as we enter the house. We settle in the living room, and I proceed to tell her about the past week. The mysterious knock on the door and the infant left outside. The fact I'd phoned the police and thought the incident was over with, only for them to follow up with me two days ago, breaking news of the unthinkable.

"Erin has a baby?" she says, her jaw dropped.

"It appears so," I say.

Mom breathes heavily for several seconds before she scoots to the edge of her seat. "Can I hold her?"

Rosie's eyes are wide, critiquing everything around her. She doesn't flinch when Mom reaches forward, unfastening the buckle of her carrier. Mom cradles the baby in her arms.

"I can't believe this," she says.

"I know," I say, watching Rosie closely. It amazes me how calm she is being handed off from one stranger to the next. If only she could embody that same contentedness in the middle of the night.

"What do the police think this means?" she asks. "About Erin."

"I don't know exactly." Frustration returns. One step forward, a dozen steps back.

"Do they think the baby belongs to Adam?"

"The police are running his DNA later today."

"That's good," Mom says, nodding along. All the information she's received about Erin's case has been filtered through me. I've given her plenty of reason to be suspicious of Adam, even if she's not as convinced of his guilt as I am.

"I'm retracing Erin's steps in the days leading to her disappearance," I say. "I've spent the past year thinking she was dead. Now there's a chance she's alive."

Mom continues staring at the baby. The smile on her face falls.

"You know, I've seen those horrible stories in the news. About women trapped in basements. Held prisoner in the woods. Forced to do things. Sometimes they have multiple children." She shivers. "I don't want to think of Erin—"

"Then don't," I say, even though I've had to fight my own imagination to keep such images at bay. "We have no reason to think that's what happened to her."

What is the likely scenario? my subconscious asks. If some kind of monstrous foul play isn't involved, then could it be what Beth suggested? Could Erin have left on her own?

Mom sits back, still holding the baby in her arms. There's a look on her face like she might be sick. "All this time I thought she was dead. That's why I never said anything."

"Said anything about what?" I ask.

"A few months ago," she says. "I got a call."

"A call?"

She nods. "It was from someone claiming to be Erin."

I sit up straighter, fear slicing through my spine. "What?"

"It was the middle of the night. My phone received a call from a unidentified number. I answered, and there was this heavy breathing on the line. I couldn't make out what they were saying at first. And then I heard it. She said, 'Mom.'"

I'm frozen still, trying to follow what she's saying. "Did it sound like Erin?"

"The line was too staticky, like there was poor service. All I could hear was a woman's voice saying, 'Mom. Help.'"

I can almost imagine Erin's voice in my mind. Shaken and afraid. Once again, it's like she's right in front of me but I can't reach her. My heart shatters.

"What did the police say?" My words are hurried, struggling to keep my emotions at bay. "Were they able to trace the call?"

"I never told the police."

My brow furrows. "What do you mean you didn't tell the police?"

"I... I thought it was a prank call."

The sorrow I felt moments ago is replaced with outrage. It's difficult for me to control my anger. "Why would you think that?"

"You seemed so sure Erin was dead. I figured you were right."

"But if she was calling you—"

"I didn't know it was her calling," she says. "I thought it was a prank."

"A prank!"

"You don't watch crime shows. People do that sort of thing! They call the families of victims just to mess with them. They think it's funny. Or it could have been one of those scams you see all over the news."

I close my eyes tight in frustration. "Either way, it's something you should have let the police look into."

"How? It was an unknown number."

I rub my forehead, struggling to voice my feelings. Mom has always been a paranoid woman, a nosy woman. Her excessive drinking keeps her prisoner in her own mind, forcing her to neglect what really matters. I can remember her calling the police because our neighbor didn't retrieve their garbage cans in a timely manner, complaining because cars on the sidewalk had overstayed their toll time, all while Erin and I went to sleep night after night without dinner.

Something of importance actually happens to her, concerning her missing daughter, and she does nothing about it. A flash of jealousy rattles through me. If Erin had a moment to call for help, why would she even consider reaching out to our mother? She should have called me.

"I can't believe you didn't tell the police," I say. "Or me."

"If it was a prankster, there was no sense in worrying you over it. You already had your hands tied up with Erin. Like always."

"What's that supposed to mean?"

My mother sighs. "You've always been too involved with

her. I mean, I'm the mother here. And yet you act like you have ownership over her. Don't you think it's odd the police come to you with all the information over me?"

"I'm the closest person to her. I always have been, when you were too busy with other things."

"I was never too busy."

It irritates me how she acts, rewriting the history of our childhood, our family. Rosie begins to wriggle in Mom's lap, causing her to grip her more tightly. She starts to cry.

"Let me have her," I say, reaching out my hands.

"Oh, so you don't like what I'm saying and you're going to take my granddaughter? Punish me?"

"She needs to be comforted," I say, removing Rosie from her arms and resting her on my chest. I feel an instant sense of protection. "Don't make any of this about you."

"It is about me!" she shouts. "My daughter is missing. I have a granddaughter I never knew about. And all you want to do is rehash the past and blame everything on me."

Now that she's getting agitated, her voice carries. Her breath crosses the distance between us, tinged with the unmistakable scent of liquor. She's drunk. Again. I should have known better, should have asked her if she was sober before I ever let her hold Rosie. Gritting my teeth, I lean forward, resting the baby inside her carrier.

"You should have told the police when Erin called you."

"And tell them what? That I'd received a call from a dead girl?"

"We know now she wasn't dead then. It could have been her, and that phone call could have let us find her."

Once Rosie is strapped in, I stand, hauling her to the front door.

"When are you going to bring her back to see me?" Mom says.

"I don't know," I say. "The first thing you need to do is call the police."

"Typical," Mom says, sitting back on the couch. "Always making me the bad guy."

I can't believe that after all this time she still can't see it, how her selfishness interferes with the well-being of her children. Erin reached out to her. If she was being held captive, it could have been her chance to escape. Because Mom didn't tell the police, we lost the opportunity to even follow up on the call.

And yet, she doesn't seem to even care about that. She just wants an excuse to be around Rosie.

For once, Byron was wrong, I think with bitter glee. Maybe she did deserve to know about her granddaughter, but after this visit, it's all I intend to share with her for a very long while.

# SIXTEEN

I'm struggling to get Rosie's carrier out of the car.

It doesn't matter how many times I pull on the strap, the seat won't budge. It's amazing that we've managed to send people to the moon, but when it comes to infant car seats, they're a bulky, complicated mess. Rosie was asleep, but all my jostling woke her up, and now she's crying. Again.

Frustration doesn't accurately sum up how I feel. The car seat situation is annoying, but the confrontation I just had with my mother goes deeper than that. I feel betrayed by her, always have. I've written her off countless times over the years as paranoid, a drunk. Still, I let her back in, give her another chance, only to be disappointed yet again.

After one last yank, whatever stubborn mechanism was in place gives, and the car seat moves. Muscles sore from lack of sleep, I haul the carrier into the house. Once inside, I'm stricken by how quiet it is, apart from Rosie's screaming, of course. The setting serves as a reminder of just how much my life has changed in the past year. In the past two days, particularly.

A place that used to be filled with so much love—weekends spent drinking wine with Erin and Viv, nights spent in bed with

Byron—is now depleted. Everything looks the same, save for a few items Byron took with him to the new apartment, but the sense of home has changed. The warmth and music of the place is gone. As I stand alone in this quiet house, my niece wailing from the carrier beside me, I can't quite believe this is my life.

I'm ashamed to admit my first instinct is to call Byron. It's not fair to him to go running back whenever I need his assistance, but he is a total natural with the baby, and he insisted he was happy to help as much as I needed.

Moving over to the sofa, I take a seat, bending forward to unstrap Rosie. Thankfully, the straps release with ease, allowing me to retrieve the squirming baby. Her limbs spread wildly, the jerky movements letting me know just how displeased she is. Her little cheeks are red from all the pent-up aggravation. I pull her closer to me, her little body wriggling against my chest.

"It's okay, little girl," I say, straining to use a calm voice. I try again, this time managing to sound more at ease. "Everything's okay. Calm down."

I never assumed being a parent was easy. But in some regards, looking after my younger sister when I was only a child myself was easier than caring for an infant now. I'm set in my ways, and Rosie's arrival was unexpected, but I can't imagine not loving her, not trying. My thoughts return to my mother.

I've always assumed our father left because he didn't want to raise another child; my last memories of him are before Erin was born. Our mother resented us for this, as though we'd had a say on when and how we entered the world. There are a dozen different reasons why she neglected us the way she did; I've unpacked several of them over the years in therapy, creating a healthy distance to my mother as a result.

But even now, when Erin is more vulnerable than ever, our mother can't be trusted. I can't believe she received a phone call and did nothing about it. Wrote it off as a prank, another instance of paranoia. The thoughts, irritating as they are, make me cling to Rosie tighter, as though she's a bridge to my sister, a conduit to the love and nurturing we never had.

Rosie's body relaxes even more, until she's a warm little lump on my chest. Eventually, she quiets. I move her over to the pack and play, moving in slow motion, afraid one jerky movement will wake her and she'll begin crying again. Once she's safely resting on the mat, I sigh in relief.

From somewhere behind me, my phone begins to ring. The sound seems louder than ever, the happy melody echoing through the house. I rush toward the sound, trying to silence it before Rosie wakes again. I'm not even sure where I put it. I follow the sound, realizing the phone is stuffed inside one of the front pockets of the diaper bag.

I silence the call, looking over my shoulder to see if Rosie is stirring. I'm relieved to see she's still sleeping and check the screen to see who is calling. It's Byron, as if he somehow read my mind and could tell I was in the middle of a crisis.

When I answer the phone, he notes my aggravated tone immediately.

"How'd things go with your mom?" Byron asks, hesitantly.

"The visit was a total nightmare," I say. "I wish you'd never suggested it."

He sighs. "I'm sorry, Emily."

I believe him. He's witnessed a handful of awkward family interactions over the course of our marriage, and yet, he still encouraged me to go. Tell her about Erin, and her grandchild. Byron always expects people to do the right thing, even when it goes against their nature.

"How did she react to the news?"

"It doesn't matter," I say. "After what she's done, I'm not giving her a chance to be in her granddaughter's life."

I go into further detail, explaining that my mother admitted to receiving a phone call from someone claiming to be Erin, and did nothing.

"Unbelievable," he says. "I should have gone with you."

"That's not your place," I say, even though my first thought is that I wish I hadn't had to deal with Mom on my own. And hadn't he been the first person I wanted to call after I left?

There's an awkward pause on the phone. The two of us are still trying to figure out what we are to each other, set new boundaries. Rosie's arrival has only complicated that.

"I wanted to give you space," he says, "but I'm still working from home, if you need me to come over."

Across the room, I watch as the baby sleeps, the gentle rise and fall of her small chest. After the frustration of visiting my mother and getting Rosie settled, we've reached a level of calm. Part of me doesn't want to disturb that.

Another part of my mind is elsewhere, across town at the police station. Adam is scheduled to be there to give a DNA sample, and the idea of sitting here placid on the couch, waiting to get a phone call from Detective Carson, makes my skin crawl.

"I could do with running by the office," I say. "If you don't mind coming over."

"Are you sure?"

I'm not sure how to answer the question. He offered to help; maybe he was only saying that to be polite. Or maybe he's judging me for going into work at a time like this. I can't tell him the truth, that I really want to check Adam is at the police station. As usual, he'd reprimand me for meddling.

"If you're busy, don't worry—"

"I'm not," he says, eagerly. "I can be there in five."

Good, I think as I hang up the phone.

Half an hour later, I'm in my car, sipping on an iced coffee. Byron arrived quickly. Rosie remained asleep, making the transition easy. Walking out of the house and entering the quiet of my car felt like slipping into a different skin, a call back to simpler times when my every thought and action didn't revolve around Rosie.

Still, it surprised me, that slight pang in my chest I felt before driving away. It's like a part of me was being left behind. Even though I trust Byron, having her out of my sight feels risky. Moments earlier, I'd been hoping for an escape, but the guilt from leaving was heavy.

I wonder if that's how parents feel all the time.

I push the sentimental feelings away so that I can focus on what's important now: Adam.

For a year, he's been able to keep the police—and me—at bay. Once we're able to prove he's the father of Erin's baby, there will be no denying the fact he's involved, and it will prove he had motive to take my sister. If he was willing to keep her alive long enough for the baby to be born, maybe she's still out there, waiting to be found.

I am parked across the street, watching as people enter and exit the small police station. A row of cruisers are parked out front, and there's a small statue of an eagle in the courtyard. Before Erin went missing, I only visited this place for work; now, I've been here more times than I can count.

I take another swig of my drink and check the time. According to what Detective Carson said, Adam should be arriving any minute. I'm not sure exactly what I plan on doing. I can't very well follow him inside the police station; Carson's already given me a warning to stay away from him.

Just seeing him will give me a sense of comfort. At least that's been the case for the past year. I may not be able to prove his involvement, I may not be able to get revenge, but I'm getting closer, and that's all that matters.

My phone rings, my initial thoughts going to Byron and something being wrong with the baby. I'm surprised to see Beth's name flash across the screen. Our conversation at the apartment didn't exactly end on the best of terms.

"I'm not happy about how things went yesterday," she says when I answer the phone.

"I agree," I admit.

"I wasn't trying to blame Erin."

And yet, it felt like that was exactly what she was doing. Even insinuating that Erin left on her own accord denies her victimhood. For a year, I've believed she was the victim of foul play. I believed she was dead. Foolishly, I thought everyone else agreed with me. Now, I wonder what other theories concerning her disappearance exist.

"You don't need to apologize," I tell her. "You can't help how you feel."

"All I care about is finding out what happened," she says.

That response still implies that she could have left on her own, a suggestion that irritates me.

"There's something else. The reason I'm calling," she says. "Something strange happened after you left."

"Strange?"

"It can't really be a coincidence." She pauses. "When I left the apartment last night I saw Adam."

Hearing his name makes my entire spine go rigid with alarm. "At the bar?"

"No. He was outside our building," she says. "It's like he was scoping out the place."

"What do you mean?"

"He was just on the sidewalk. He must not have noticed me at first," she says. "When he finally saw me, he turned around like he didn't want to be seen."

"Did you say anything to him?"

"I tried. He just kept walking," she says. "I've not seen him since before Erin went missing. It can't be a coincidence that he shows up the same day you come by, right?"

I agree. What are the odds he'd start hanging around her apartment again right after Rosie shows up?

"Anyway, I know you think he's involved," she says. "I thought you needed to know."

"Thank you," I say, getting off the phone, anger pulsating inside me.

There's no telling how many hours I've spent following him in the past year, and now the tables are turned, and he's doing his own investigation. If he is holding Erin somewhere, maybe he's trying to keep tabs on the baby. Maybe he's the person who left Rosie on my doorstep in the first place.

The police station doors open. A man exits the building, waltzing past the bronze eagle statue. I recognize him immediately.

But it isn't Adam. It's David, Erin's former teacher's assistant. The one who got fired because of her.

# SEVENTEEN

I blink several times, trying to make sense of what I'm seeing.

It's been years since I've seen David in the flesh. Most recently, I found the pictures from his social media. New life in a different state, a beautiful wife and two small kids.

He looks different from the young teaching assistant I remember from years ago. His hair is thinning and graying at the sides, a byproduct of fatherhood, I'm sure. Or maybe there's another reason he's been under stress in recent years.

Why is he here?

Before I have time to consider more questions, I'm out of my car, following him across the street.

"David?" Part of me hopes he'll ignore my call, that I'm mistaken and it's some stranger walking in front of me.

Instead, David turns to face me, squinting. I can't tell if it's confusion, or if the bright sun is affecting his vision.

"David Strange?" I ask, as I get closer. "From East Marshall University?"

"Sorry." He looks back at the police station, and then his car, before giving me his full attention. "Do I know you?"

I can't blame him for not remembering me. As I recall, I

only met him once, when I was in the process of helping Erin move.

"I'm Emily March," I say. "Erin's sister."

At the mention of her name, his entire demeanor changes. He becomes shifty, unsure.

"Look, I already did everything the police asked," he says.

"What exactly did the police ask?" I respond, confused.

"They wanted me to submit a DNA sample."

I'm surprised by his answer. As far as I knew, he hadn't been in contact with Erin in a decade. Detective Carson never mentioned there were any other suspects during yesterday's visit.

"So much has happened in the past few days, I'm struggling to keep up," I say. "Why exactly did the police ask you to do that?"

"They haven't talked to you?" he asks.

Not about him. My entire focus has been on Adam. I shake my head.

He sighs, looking up and down the street again, as though he expects someone to interrupt us. "They contacted me a few days ago. They want to rule me out as the father of Erin's baby."

"But why?" I ask. "I know you have history, but that was ages ago."

"I told them that. I've not seen Erin in years." He pauses. "But we had reconnected on social media. Nothing major. I mean, I'm happily married. We'd just exchange messages from time to time. Catch up with one another."

"What kinds of messages?" I ask, almost afraid to hear the answer.

"It wasn't anything like that," he says, his pitch turning suspiciously high. "I guess the police considered the conversation flirtatious, but it was just catching up. Things ended so suddenly between us all those years ago. I guess part of me wanted to know if she turned out okay, like I did."

"How long had you been talking to Erin?" I ask.

"About six months. She reached out to me after her most recent breakup. Some guy named Adam." At the sound of his name, my heart stills. "We only messaged back and forth for a little while. I didn't even realize she was reported missing at first. I just figured she'd stopped making contact."

"So, you stopped talking before she went missing?"

"Yeah. I only found out after the police reached out to me. I guess they'd seen our texts."

I can't believe they were in contact at all. Rather, I can't believe Erin didn't tell me about it. Of course, she probably feared I'd reprimand her. The fiasco with David was one of the first major setbacks in her adult life, and I encouraged her to put as much distance between herself and him as possible, the same way I warned her about Adam years later.

"Really, I think they just wanted to rule me out," he says. "And, to be honest, I wanted to cooperate to keep this whole thing quiet. I didn't do anything inappropriate with Erin, but I don't really want my wife knowing I'm chatting online with an old girlfriend."

I can imagine that not going over well. Then again, if it were only a few innocent messages, I can't believe the police would make him travel all the way here.

"Are you sure you didn't meet up with her in person?"

He narrows his eyes at me, annoyed. "I already told you."

"When do they expect to get results?"

He shrugs. "I don't know, but I'm not worried about it. Like I said, there's no way I'm the father." He pauses. "By then, I'm hoping to be back home with my family. The last thing I need is Erin blowing up my life for a second time."

There's a bitterness in his tone that strikes me. Even if what he says about being happy now is true, he lost his job and damaged his reputation dating an undergrad. I wonder if he's harbored resentment for Erin all these years. Maybe they reconnected more closely than he's willing to admit, and he used the reunion as an opportunity to get back at her for everything she'd taken from him.

"I'm sorry about what happened to your sister," he says. "But I had nothing to do with it and I just want to go back to my life."

I don't say anything else. I move over to the sidewalk, watching as he gets into his car and pulls away. Part of me is stunned to have seen him here, but another part of me is angry at Erin all over again.

David is yet another secret she kept from me. She would have known I wouldn't want her talking to him again. Not to mention, he's married. Even if their conversations were platonic, as he claims, it's inappropriate to message a married man given their history.

All this time I thought we told each other everything, but Erin clearly concealed the choices she thought I wouldn't approve of. It was never my intention to make her feel judged, but I realize now my reactions to her past mistakes might have contributed to the pile of secrets she kept from me. It's why I don't have all the details needed to find her now.

I turn around to walk back in the direction of my car, when I catch sight of someone else standing by the bronze statue.

This time it's the person I've been waiting for. Adam. And he's looking right at me, his gaze full of contempt.

# EIGHTEEN

*Go back to your car*, a voice inside me says. I imagine a little angel on my shoulder, trying desperately to diffuse the situation.

But the devil on the other side is stronger and bigger and louder, fueled by the pent-up grief I've been harboring for a year. Before I know it, I'm crossing the street, walking straight toward Adam.

For a moment, he's as still as the eagle statue up ahead, his gaze fixed on me, as if he's as stunned. When he does move, it's quick. He turns around, retreating in the direction of the police station.

I think of all the times I've watched him in silence, nothing more than a shadow following his every move.

Something about being this close to him, knowing he's seen me, urges me to confront him.

"Adam!" I shout after him, before he can make it into the building. My volume is loud enough it catches the attention of a few pedestrians on the sidewalk, but I don't care. I keep moving. "Don't be a coward. Talk to me."

"That's not why I'm here," he says quietly, as though he's fighting his own internal struggle over whether to engage.

"I know why you're here," I say. "You fathered Erin's baby. The DNA test will confirm it, and then we'll be able to prove you murdered her."

There's something about yelling the word *murdered* in broad daylight, in the middle of a public street. The passersby who only moments ago tried to ignore us stand still, transfixed by the spectacle in front of them. Normally, I'd be mindful of their stares, their judgements, but at this moment, I don't care.

"You were the last person with her," I taunt him. "Her blood was found in your car. I know all about your little drives out into the woods. Is that where you left her, Adam? Is that where she's buried?"

I've laid out the facts to countless people in the past year. Byron. The police. Marco. Anyone who will listen. But I've never confronted Adam directly. I tell myself I haven't been given the chance, but maybe that's not true. Perhaps I didn't have the courage until now.

Everything I've uncovered in the past few days fuels me forward. I'm closer than ever to finding out the truth about what happened, and all I want him to do is admit it. I think of Rosie back home, how much Erin deserves to be there with her instead of me. And yet, she's not.

Because of him.

"Are you the one who left the baby on my doorstep?" I ask him as he starts moving away. "Did you abandon your own daughter?"

That comment shakes him more than all the others. He halts his forward march, turns around to face me.

"I'm not the father."

"Of course you are. Who else could it be?"

Even though I've just found out they're testing other people, as David revealed, I don't care. David hasn't been on my radar. Neither has anyone else. Adam is the only person who has a recent complicated history with my sister. He knows what happened to her. I'm sure of it.

"After all this time, can't you just tell me?" I say, my anger waning slightly, turning into pleading. "Just tell me the truth."

Adam opens his mouth to speak, but before he can say anything, the gleaming glass doors to the police station open wide, and Detective Carson comes outside. One of the startled onlookers must have gone inside for help, or maybe my desperate words were loud enough for them to hear indoors.

"You have no business being here," Detective Carson says, pointing his finger at me. He flicks his eyes over to Adam. "Go inside."

"I'm only asking him questions," I say, stepping forward, wanting to chase after him. He was close to telling me something, and I want to know what it is. "I want to know what happened to Erin."

"This is not the way to get answers," Carson says, blocking my path. He stares down at me, waiting for Adam to go inside, the doors drifting shut behind him. "I told you about the testing because you wanted updates about the case. I was not giving you permission to harass people."

"You use that word a lot, don't you?"

This isn't the first time Detective Carson has warned me to stop harassing Adam. I think of his threat after I plastered those missing persons flyers outside the secondhand shop. I only ever got better at hiding my contempt; I never stopped following him.

"None of this is helping us find your sister."

"This is the closest we've ever been to finding out the truth. The baby proves she was alive five months ago. She was being kept somewhere. Maybe she still is. All this time, you've said there isn't enough evidence to tie Adam to her disappearance, but now there is."

"We won't know that until we get the results of the DNA test." He looks back at the building. "If Adam is still willing to cooperate, that is."

My stomach turns over in shame. I hadn't considered that my confrontation would scare Adam into not participating. If he refuses to volunteer a sample, it could take even longer to get answers. I should have waited to confront him until he was leaving, but seeing him here, this close to me, made it impossible to walk away.

"How long will it take to get results?"

"Anywhere from twenty-four to forty-eight hours," he says. "We'll let you know as soon as the results are in. You need to stay away from here. Stay away from Adam. And leave the investigation to us."

"I didn't know you were testing other people, too," I say, thinking of my conversation with David. "Why didn't you tell me?"

"You think I want you causing a public scene with every person on our suspect list?"

"There is no suspect list—"

"To you, there isn't. That's your problem. This entire year the only name on your list has been Adam's. I don't know, maybe he is to blame. But if someone else is involved, you haven't done yourself any favors in focusing only on him."

It doesn't make sense that it could be anyone else. All the evidence points to him. I know how he treated her, how being with him put Erin at risk. It's like dealing with the instability of our mother all over again.

I left my sister at the restaurant that night, knowing Adam was waiting for her, and proving his involvement with whatever happened to her is the only way I can make up for that mistake.

"Go home," Detective Carson repeats. "You're lucky I'm not arresting you."

"Oh yeah. Lucky me."

"There's a baby you're responsible for now. That's why I'm letting you leave," he says. "But if I see you here again, you'll be in custody, and Erin's daughter will go back into the system."

That last threat physically hurts. I never thought about how my actions might impact others. How my mistakes could jeopardize Rosie's future. I'm all she has left.

My cheeks are red as I turn around and walk in the direction of my car.

# NINETEEN

## ERIN

The Night of the Disappearance

Emily has the best laugh. Not the polite, controlled one she offers up when others are around. The hearty, wild one that rings out when she's with me, reverberating around us.

We're not exactly alone, but despite the crowded restaurant, it feels like it's just the two of us, as it always has been. Her volume increases with each sip of wine, and I can't stop thinking about how amazing it is to be together like this. I'm going to miss these moments.

Then he appears, a physical manifestation of my dread. I told him to wait for me in the car, that I'd be out in time, but he never listens. He's just so intense. Constantly watching over me and looking out for me, especially since he's come back into my life.

Emily knows this, and it's why she can't stand him. I watch as the joy in her face dulls, listen as the gaiety in her voice fades. I'm already missing my sister from seconds ago, wishing I could bring her back.

"What are you doing here?" she asks him, that sharp edge to her voice.

"Erin and I have plans," he says. His tone is always short when he speaks to her, eyes on me, as though nothing else in the world exists.

I gave him a look, pleading with him to bite his tongue. They never got along. It's one of the reasons I decided to break up, but things are different now. I'm hoping, moving forward, they'll be able to accept each other, but that won't happen if they fight. They go back and forth, each of them trying to prove they have more control over me.

"It's fine, Emily. We made plans for later. We were just about to have dessert," I tell him. "Please, just wait in the car."

He remains motionless for a minute, as though he hasn't decided how to react. I watch as he checks the time on his wristwatch, impatiently stomps his feet.

"Ten minutes," he says, hands in pockets, before weaving through the patio tables, back toward the street.

"Sorry about that," I say to Emily, trying to resurrect the easy happiness that had existed before his arrival.

"You said the two of you broke up," she says.

"We did," I say. "He's only here as a friend."

Emily scoffs, that critical sound that makes me feel like a thousand ants are crawling all over me. There's no worse place to be than in the midst of her judgement.

"Don't lie to me. Exes can't be friends," she says, bitterly. "Especially after everything he put you through."

"He's getting better."

"Do you know how ridiculous you sound?" Emily spits. "How many times did Mom get better over the years?"

Emily knows my greatest wounds, and when she's angry, she can't stop herself from cutting deep. Our mother's drinking hurt both of us, but Emily's older, has worse memories. She doesn't understand that he's different from Mom, even if they're controlled by the same vice.

"You need to trust me," I say. "I know what I'm doing."

I always seek my sister's approval. Her opinion matters more to me than anyone else's, and nothing makes me feel smaller than when I know I've let her down. She has this way of looking at me, her judgements and opinions picking me apart. I don't think it's intentional, but sometimes I wonder. If she knew the truth about everything I'd done, there's a good chance she'd never speak to me again, something that would be worse than everything else.

Emily finishes the last of her wine and stands, but not without hitting me with one last jab. "If you want me to trust you, stop making stupid choices."

"Please, Emily." I stand quickly, the desperation in my voice so unlike me. Our night wasn't supposed to end like this. We were meant to have a happy dinner. I need her to have good thoughts about me before what happens next.

"It's fine, really," she says. I can see that she's trying to control her irritation. She doesn't like fighting any more than I do, and I hate that it always seems to be me causing tension between us. "Just call me later. Let me know you made it home, all right?"

My stomach drops. I know I'm not going to be calling her. That isn't part of the plan. I'd thought this dinner would buy me a few days. She's going to be worried when she doesn't hear from me.

I sit down just as the waitress brings our dessert. A chocolate cake with extra whipped cream and two spoons. The sight of it makes my stomach turn. I think about my sister. I think about him.

My head in my hands, I wonder, when did it become this easy to let so many people down?

# TWENTY

## EMILY

When I return home, I make an excuse to get Byron out of the house. He'd be furious if he knew where I'd really been, even more upset if he learned my confrontation with Adam earned me another tongue-lashing from Detective Carson.

"I can stay for dinner, if you'd like," he says, as I'm walking him out the door. "Rosie basically slept the whole time you were gone. She might give you a hard night."

"I'll be fine," I say. "You've done enough."

Between the argument with my mother and everything that happened at the police station, I'm frazzled, and I don't need to wrestle with my guilty emotions about Byron.

Within minutes of him leaving, Rosie begins to cry. I prepare a bottle and we settle in on the sofa. She takes the formula greedily, staring up at me with big, round eyes. Detective Carson's warning comes back to me. If I continue making rash decisions, I could lose Rosie.

Right now, she's all I have left.

The way people look at me—the way I look at myself—has changed in the past year. My marriage is completely ruined. I would have had more repercussions at work if it weren't for

Viv. She's lenient with me, far more than a typical boss would be.

All I ever wanted was to uncover the truth, but my desperation to do so pushed everyone away. I think of the way Beth treated me earlier in the week, like I was some fragile grenade on the verge of detonation.

Then again, maybe it's my own actions, my own failures, that have brought me to this point.

Last winter, I dreaded the impending season because it would be my first round of holidays without my sister. Every cheery song on the radio or sparkling decoration on a front lawn tempted me to curse.

Byron's newspaper always throws an epic holiday party, but I wasn't up for attending. Byron kept begging, reminding me how important it was to him that I come. Told me it would be good to take my mind off things.

*Things* meaning my sister. Her death.

I told him I'd go just to shut him up. I convinced myself I could put in a one-hour appearance for him. For us. But when the time came, and I saw myself in the mirror wearing a ridiculous sequined dress, I couldn't bear to follow through.

Byron, who was already at the event setting up, called a dozen times that night. I never had the courage to answer. I wasn't much in the mood for being home alone either, waiting for the inevitable fight once he returned.

I got in my car and drove to Adam's apartment instead. I spent the night sipping hot coffee in my car, watching him through his window, wondering if his holidays were as glum as mine. Wondering if he had any remorse for what he'd taken from me.

When I finally came home, Byron was already there. I knew he was upset because he didn't even wait for me. He'd gone straight to bed, like he didn't have the energy for an argument.

I was standing in the kitchen when I saw it. A plaque

displaying gold and crimson script. Byron had been named Journalist of the Year by his colleagues. He'd been awarded it that very night, and I'd missed it. Stalking Adam and ruminating over my own regrets was more important than being there for my husband.

That night was the beginning of the end for us. He took on an assignment in January that sent him to California for two weeks—the longest we'd ever been apart. The most unsettling part of his absence was how little I missed him.

I squeeze Rosie a little tighter, relishing in the warmth of her skin against mine. I have to start putting others before myself, before Erin.

Rosie deserves better.

* * *

The next morning, I'm sitting in front of my living room window, waiting eagerly for the mailman to arrive. Marco's article about Erin releases today. When I do finally get my hands on the newspaper, as expected, the article is written beautifully, my former co-worker having kept his promise to bring as much attention as possible to the case.

When I sat down with him a few days ago, I hoped this article would put pressure on the police to make an arrest. Now, the investigation has changed entirely. Rosie is in the picture, and all I can think about is what the DNA tests might reveal. Erin could still be out there, being kept prisoner.

Or, with a shudder, I wonder if the police are thinking along the same lines as Beth, that Erin's disappearance was intentional.

That was the point of the article. If you get enough people in the community interested in a case, it forces the police to make decisions, reconsider avenues they previously wrote off.

After reading the article, I go to the internet, to see if there's already chatter about Erin.

There are a few groups I follow, most of them local true crime clubs. Even though the majority of conversations revolve around nationally famous cases, local connections pique interest. Sure enough, there are a few comments referring to Erin and the fact she's been missing for a year. Some people go through their theories again, but there's nothing new or substantial. A handful of people agree with Beth's version of events, that Erin simply walked away from her life. No one mentions the baby.

Rosie is in the bassinet, sleeping. When it comes to the public, I'm conflicted about what her appearance could mean for Erin's case. If the community knew that Erin had a child, it would definitely get people interested again. Like me, they'd wonder how a missing woman—one who many people believed to be dead—had a child. That's the former reporter in me, chasing a good story that would engage readers.

The sister in me, and I guess the aunt, wants Rosie's existence to remain a secret. I don't want anyone to know who she is, or that I have her, for fear it could put her in further danger.

My confrontation with Adam plays on a loop in my mind, every detail, from the excitement that rushed through me when I first saw him, to the way he looked as though he were about to finally say something, just before we were interrupted.

I recall what Detective Carson said, too. That my intense focus on Adam could be leaving room for other people to go unnoticed. But who else would want to hurt Erin?

The doorbell rings. Viv has stopped by on her lunch break again. When I open the door, I see she has a takeout bag in her hands.

"Is it your mission to keep me fed?"

"It's the least I can do," she says. "I'm worried about you.

And the baby. I want to make sure you have everything you need."

The sound of Viv's voice carries through the house, acting as an alarm for Rosie. I see her start to wriggle in the bassinet, my body moaning in exhaustion as I hurry to reach for her.

"You eat," Viv tells me, reading my mind. "I can handle the baby."

I'm relieved I have a moment to be still. Viv lifts her from the bassinet, and I see Rosie's splayed fingers reaching for the ends of Viv's hair. "Have you decided what to call her?" she asks.

"Byron has been calling her Rosie," I say.

"That's cute," Viv says, gently hopping the baby on her hip. "Where is Byron?"

I shrug, carrying the bag of takeout to the kitchen counter. The delicious smells of seasoning hit the air as I pull out the food and unwrap the sandwich. I take a bite, my mouth watering.

"Hasn't he been helping you?" she asks.

"I actually can take care of her on my own," I say. "Don't get me wrong. I appreciate his help. Byron's doing what he always does, but it isn't fair to him. We're not together anymore. I can't expect him to drop whatever he's doing for me."

"He said he took off the rest of the week."

"Maybe he's catching up on sleep," I say. "Lord knows I could use some."

"Are the nights that bad?" Viv says, looking at Rosie as though she could never be the source of my annoyance.

To be fair, my lack of sleep isn't all because of the baby. It's only been a couple of days, but we're starting to fall into a routine. I have a sense of what calms her, what doesn't. I know what times to give her a bottle so that she'll sleep soundly for a couple of hours.

The problem is, even after Rosie nods off, I'm wide awake.

"I'm driving myself crazy thinking about Erin," I say.

I fill Viv in on everything that's happened in the past couple of days, my conversations with Beth and my mother, followed by my confrontations with Adam and David at the police station.

"You know your sister better than anyone," she says when I finish. "If you think Adam is involved, you should trust your gut."

I nod, pointing to the newspaper on the coffee table. "The article was supposed to bring more attention to Erin's case. Maybe someone will come forward."

"Did you tell the police what your mother said about receiving a phone call from Erin?"

"I was so flustered once I saw Adam, I didn't even think about it." My phone begins pinging somewhere on the sofa. I feel around for it, checking to see who sent a message. My heart beats faster when I scan the words on the screen. "This could be my chance."

"Who is it?" she asks, readjusting Rosie in her arms.

"It's Detective Carson," I say. "The DNA test results are in."

# TWENTY-ONE

I shuffle to the back of the house and pull open the sliding glass doors. Sharp sunlight stings my eyes, as does the sensory overload of itchy pollen and pungent soil. Perhaps I'm more tired than I realized, or maybe I'm feeling overstimulated due to the adrenaline coursing through me.

This is it. After an entire year, something concrete could tie Adam to Erin's disappearance, a clear motive as to why he would want her out of the way.

The phone rings twice before Detective Carson answers. The sound of his voice makes me feel like my heart will drop out of my chest.

"Normally, we'd deliver news like this in person," he says, "but that would take more time. I assumed you'd want to know straight away."

He's right. I'm sick of the stalling. "Tell me, please. What are the results?"

"Adam is not biologically related to the child."

My heart drops further, somewhere beyond my reach, shattering into a million pieces. That can't be right.

"He has to be," I say. "Nothing else makes sense."

Every muscle in my body turns rigid and I feel an irrational need to defend what I believe. Adam is the person responsible for this, always has been.

If he's not Rosie's father, I have to reconsider everything. There's a tightness in my chest at the possibility I could have gotten this wrong, that what the police and Byron and even Adam himself has been trying to tell me could be true.

"I can assure you the test is accurate," he says. "I know this isn't what you wanted to hear—"

"Are you sure?" I ask, cutting him off. I'm desperate for a different answer, a different outcome.

"Yes. The child is related to Erin, related to you, but not Adam."

I can almost sense pity in his voice. Carson and I have had some tense exchanges over the past year, but he knows better than anyone how much I wanted this. Or maybe I'm only imagining his sympathy.

"What about David?" I ask. "I saw him at the police station yesterday. I know you tested him, too."

"We're still waiting on his results."

"Why would his take longer?"

"The lab runs on its own timeframe," he says. "We'll get results when we can, and let you know."

Or maybe the preliminary results weren't what they were expecting. Maybe David is the baby's father, and they're re-testing the sample to make sure. There's a soreness in my chest. I'd been surprised to see David at all, never really considered he could be the father. But I feel completely defeated by the fact that yesterday there were two possible suspects, and now there's nothing.

"Have you tested anyone else?" I ask, wondering if perhaps there is someone else on their radar.

"Not at this time," he says, "but I can promise you we're doing everything we can to further our investigation."

More of the same empty promises I've heard over and over. Even if the police are trying, it isn't enough. Erin has a child. She could still be out there. It feels like she's just beyond my reach and a million miles away all at once.

I end the phone call, defeated. We're no closer to finding out where Erin could be, and I'm embarrassed that my intuition about Adam could be so off. It doesn't make sense. Even if he's not Rosie's father, he could still be involved, though. Maybe that's why he harmed Erin, took her, because he knew she'd moved on with someone else. But who?

I recall our confrontation yesterday. He'd been on the verge of telling me something, and I need to know what that is.

"What did they say?" Viv asks me as soon as I step back inside.

Rosie wrestles in her arms, as Viv tries to keep her composure. She must be just as anxious to hear the news as I was.

"Adam isn't the father," I say, ripping off the Band-Aid.

"What?" She sounds as heartbroken as I feel. "Are they sure?"

"Yes, they're sure."

"I'm so sorry, Emily," Viv says, forcing herself to look away from me and at Rosie. "I know this isn't what you wanted."

I can't even process. I need space and time to think. More information.

"I was thinking about running by the police station," I tell her. "Talk some more with Detective Carson."

"Okay," Viv says, bouncing the baby on her knee.

"You think you can handle Rosie?"

Viv's eyes bulge. "Me? I have work."

"You're the boss, remember? Call Matt and tell him to manage things."

Viv looks between Rosie and me. "You trust me to watch her?"

"Of course I do," I say, walking. "You're my best friend. I trust you with everything."

Except telling her the truth about where I'm going. If she knew I was tracking down Adam on my own, she would try to stop me.

* * *

I'm no stranger to Adam's apartment. I've spied on this location countless times from the safety of my own car. But I must admit, stepping out in the middle of the day and walking to his building, knocking on the door, is a different sensation. Fear worms through me, the unknown presenting a threat. At the same time, I feel powerful, taking control in a way I've not been able to do before.

I've spent the past year grieving, not only because I believed Erin died, but because I feared I'd never be able to prove it. Now that Rosie is here, I can ask questions and demand answers. And Detective Carson, or anyone else, won't be able to stop me.

The front door swings open. Adam is stunned, his eyes two wide saucers. He pushes the door forward, as though he's about to close it in my face, but then he pauses.

"What are you doing here?" he asks.

Without skipping a beat, I say, "You aren't the father of Erin's baby."

"I know. The police called me, too." He smirks a little. "I told you I had nothing to do with Erin's disappearance. I've been telling you that."

"I want to talk about Erin," I say. "You know something. And I need to know what it is."

He steps back, pushing the door wider. "Come inside."

"I don't think so." I nod to the gazebo that sits in the center of his apartment building's yard. "Let's sit over here."

The last thing I plan on doing is being alone with Adam. I'm still mostly certain he murdered my sister or is holding her captive somewhere. He's involved somehow.

"Give me five minutes," he says, shutting the door in my face.

A couple minutes later, we're walking in the direction of the gazebo, an awkward energy pulsating between us.

"Beth said she saw you outside her apartment," I begin.

"Erin has been on my mind a lot lately, even before all this. It's been a year since she left." He pauses, rubs the back of his neck. "I read your interview in the newspaper."

The one-year anniversary. This was the most significant event in my life. And then Rosie arrived.

"Then, out of the blue, I get a phone call from the police asking me to submit DNA for a paternity test. They told me about the baby at your house."

Adam turns to face me. He's gone pale, wearing the same expression from yesterday, before we were interrupted by Detective Carson. He raises his hand and begins rubbing his forehead, as though he's trying to add some color and life back to his draining body.

"At the very least, Erin was alive up until a few months ago. She could still be alive, but for some reason, her baby was left on my doorstep in the middle of the night. Either someone else left the baby, or Erin did it herself, but I know she wouldn't have done that unless she was in some type of danger." I pause, making sure he's following my every word. "If Erin is alive, she's being held somewhere."

"I've always told you she was alive," he says. "But leaving the baby behind doesn't make sense."

"All this time, I thought the two of you got into a fight. I thought you killed her." I pause. "Now I believe something else happened. I believe you've been hiding her away somewhere, and she ended up having a baby."

"That's ridiculous. We—"

"Maybe she found a way to escape. Maybe she's on the run now. Or maybe you've already done something to her and didn't have it in your heart to hurt the baby, so you left her on my doorstep," I say. "Either way, I know you're involved."

He sits down on the narrow bench, swiping his palms against his temples. I've never seen him this animated before. In the past, whenever I'd question him, he was defiant, indifferent. He knew whatever I said about him was nothing more than accusations. Now, there's no denying he's worried. After all this time, I wonder if he knows the jig is up.

He sits up straighter, resting his hands on his knees. He breathes deeply.

"Okay," he says. "It's time for me to tell you what really happened that night."

# TWENTY-TWO

## ERIN

### The Night of the Disappearance

Rain sprinkles over my shoulders as I exit the restaurant. The wind picks up, bringing with it a cold chill. I pull my jacket around me, walking into the dark parking garage.

I'm still unsettled about how things turned out with Emily. I'm never at peace when I'm arguing with my sister, and after everything that's happened recently, that's all I want. Peace.

Headlights flick on ahead, forcing me to squint and stand still. I raise my hand, blocking the brightness to get a better look. I recognize the car immediately. As I walk toward it, my feet stumble over something uneven on the ground. Sharp pain needles the side of my foot.

I stop walking, using the light on my phone to examine the sore spot and find a small cut. There's a jagged piece of broken glass on the ground. It must have slipped inside my shoe and done the damage.

*Great*, I think. *Tetanus is exactly what I need, on top of everything else.*

He honks the horn, the blaring sound startling me so much I

almost lose my balance again. I press my fingers against my injured foot, a smear of blood staining my fingers. I wipe my hands against my jacket as I get into the car.

"Took you long enough," he says once the door shuts.

"You didn't have to come in there, you know," I say to him, pulling the jacket tighter around me.

"We have to keep to schedule."

"I can tell time just as easily as you can," I say. "We're going to be fine."

Silence settles in, neither of us wanting to escalate the situation further. He fiddles with the radio, bouncing through staticky stations to find one that's clear. At last, he says, "Your sister always treats me like that. Like I'm beneath you, or something."

"She doesn't—"

"She does!" he cuts me off, his volume rising.

"She doesn't really know you," I say.

"And whose fault is that?"

Back when we were dating it was difficult, trying to balance the emotions of my sister and my boyfriend. The two most important people in my life were unable to get along and it was exhausting.

Not that I could tell either one of them this, but they're both right.

He can be intense, controlling. He puts up walls with everyone except for me, and that's his downfall. It's been getting better since he entered treatment, but some habits are hard to break.

Likewise, she can be too judgemental, too quick to put people into a certain category. From the moment she decided she didn't like him, he had no chance of redeeming himself.

I reach over and squeeze his forearm, feeling how he tenses beneath my touch. "It's her loss that she doesn't know you the way I do. I really appreciate what you're doing for me."

I watch his demeanor soften. He still loves me, I know this.

It's why he's willing to do anything for me. I still have feelings for him, too.

"Are you sure about this?"

I pull my hand back, fiddling with the zipper of my jacket. "I'm sure. I just wish things hadn't ended on such a weird note with Emily."

"So, what's the plan?" he asks, for what must be the dozenth time.

We go over it again, every single detail. As usual, he questions my choices and offers other solutions. Ways he can help, be there for me, but I rebuff his advances. I've come to the decision that this is for the best. If I ever want my life to improve, I must break the cycle. Break *my* cycles. I've roamed from one messed up situation to the next, convinced I could somehow save my partners from their problems. I'd never considered that I'm the one that needs fixing. If I stick around, my life and relationships will be ruined beyond repair, but if I take a little space, a little time for myself, I might finally become the woman I want to be. I'll prove Emily and everyone else wrong. Come back stronger, better. At the thought of this, my limbs tingle with possibility.

We're quiet for the rest of the car ride, as we zoom through the winding forest roads. I look out my window at the passing trees, imagine what might be going on in the darkness. When we were kids, Emily and I would go camping in our backyard. She'd always get scared after nightfall; it didn't matter that she was the older sibling. It was me who told her not to worry, to ignore the howling of wolves and coyotes in the distance, to focus on the brightness of the moon.

That's what I do now, peering at the light in the sky. It's a reminder that everything is temporary. Even the hardest of situations are nothing more than a phase. In time, another one will come along.

The isolation around us is soon replaced with streetlamps

and stoplights as we make it to the next town over. I check my watch. We're right on time; he was only being overprotective when he told me to hurry.

When we arrive at our destination, we sit in silence for several minutes. I wonder what he is thinking. Part of me doesn't want to know. Finally, he says, "I can go with you."

I sigh. "We talked about this."

"I love you, Erin," he says. "I want to know you're okay."

It would probably be less scary if I wasn't on my own, but that isn't fair to ask of him. It would only stoke the feelings I know he still has for me. I've made a lot of mistakes, but I can't be cruel in giving him false hope.

"This is for the best," I say. "You have to trust me."

I can see his dilemma. He doesn't want to trust, doesn't want to let me go. He'd do anything for me, but is it truly possible for him to let me leave?

His hand rests on the car door, and for a moment, I can't tell if he's going to exit the car, or secure the lock, trapping me inside.

# TWENTY-THREE
## EMILY

My knees feel weak as I sit down, trying not to let on just how overwhelmed I am.

For an entire year, I've wanted to know what happened to my sister. I've stayed up at night, obsessing over it. And in all those visions and fantasies, Adam was there, keeping her from me. At last, he's about to tell me the truth.

As desperate as I am to hear what he has to say, a sliver of fear runs through me. My gaze flicks over my surroundings, thankful for the daylight and the passing pedestrians. Adam won't be able to cause me any physical harm.

"Go ahead," I say, trying to maintain the strength of my voice, show that I'm in control.

Adam stands and paces the small area before sitting back down on the narrow bench across from mine. He leans forward, resting his elbows on his knees.

"I've tried telling you, there were things about Erin you didn't know."

My first instinct is to argue back; I'm so tired of people pretending I don't know my own sister. And yet, the past few days have proven that's true. I didn't know she was taking time off work. I didn't know she was in contact with David. I pinch myself to stay quiet, allowing him to speak. He needs to tell me everything.

"For starters, we never got back together. No matter what you think," he continues. "We were just friends."

That's what angered him to the point of lashing out, I think. Erin was moving on with her life. Don't they say that's the most dangerous time to leave a relationship? When the abusive partner senses the game is up, their power no longer as potent as it once was?

"Erin got into some trouble," he says. "And I was trying to help her, the way she helped me."

That response isn't one I was expecting. "What do you mean, the way she helped you?"

"My drinking," he says, locking his jaw. "That's the real reason we called it quits. I lost her, too many jobs to count, my sense of self. I needed help, and Erin was the only person who wouldn't walk away from me. She encouraged me to enter treatment."

"When?"

"Right after our breakup. I went away for thirty days. When I got back, I started meeting with a group down at the local church. I was part of the program for months before I reconnected with her."

That lines up with the timeline of their breakup. Erin didn't mention Adam at all in the months before her disappearance, and then he appeared out of nowhere that night at the restaurant. Still, I wonder how much I can trust him.

"AA encourages you to avoid romantic relationships when you're trying to get sober," I say. I remember that much from Mom's love-and-hate relationship with the program. "You shouldn't have reached out to her."

"She reached out to me as a friend," he says, confident. "Because she was in trouble."

"What kind of trouble?"

Adam sighs. "She said she'd started a new relationship and was in over her head."

"That's ridiculous," I say, the words slipping out before I can stop them. "I would know if Erin was dating someone new."

"She didn't want anyone to know," he says. "Not even you."

That doesn't make sense. We told each other everything about our lives. I knew as many details about her breakup with Adam as she did about my marriage with Byron. If she had moved on to someone else, she would have told me.

"You're lying," I say. "Why would she tell her ex-boyfriend about a new relationship over her sister?"

"We were friends. I keep telling you that," he says, moving his hands wildly. "I was devastated when we broke up, but I still cared about her. I only wanted her to be happy."

Once again, I must fight myself to keep quiet. I need to hear everything from his perspective before I can weigh in.

"She didn't tell you or anyone else about him because she was ashamed of the relationship," he continues. "I'm not sure why."

"Who was it?"

"I never knew his name. Only that things had gotten serious fast, and she was in trouble. She needed help."

"I don't understand," I say. "Help with what?"

Adam remains quiet for a long time, as though he's in a debate with himself. How much should he tell me? Will it give away too much?

"She was pregnant."

Erin knew about the baby? I'd assumed even if she was already pregnant when she disappeared that she didn't find out about the pregnancy until after she went missing. I can't believe she knew before she disappeared. And she didn't tell me about it, but she told Adam?

"I don't understand why she would tell you," I say. "Unless you were the father."

"Erin and I hadn't been intimate in a long time," he says. "The father was the guy she was dating."

So much information has been thrown at me I feel like my head is spinning.

"Why wouldn't she tell me?"

"Maybe she was ashamed. Maybe she was conflicted over what to do," he says. "Either way, she trusted me. She'd supported me when I was at my darkest moment. I was willing to help her any way I could."

"So, what happened that night?"

"I took her to the closest train station," he says. "She said she needed space. She wanted to have the baby and raise it on her own, but she couldn't do it here. She wanted to start over somewhere else."

"Start over?"

"You know Erin, always the daydreamer. Whenever she talked about the baby, she'd rattle on about starting over in a different city. Sometimes she'd talk about settling down in some cabin, becoming one with nature. I think it made her feel better, imagining a different life for herself."

Nothing he's saying makes sense. Erin was a dreamer, but running away without telling me doesn't sound like my sister at all. "You just left her and never heard from her again?"

"She reached out once," he says.

"What do you mean? When?"

"She told me she'd arrived safely and that she wasn't coming back."

"She just told you all this over a phone call?"

"It was a text message," he says. "I tried replying to the number a couple of times but never got an answer."

"And you weren't concerned? You didn't think it was odd

that she messaged you out of the blue to say she's walking away from her life?"

"Considering everything she'd been through, no," he says. "She'd gotten into a bad relationship and decided to end things. She was behind on rent, trying to make sure she had enough money to start over. And even though she never gave me all the details, I could tell she was deeply ashamed."

"She had no reason to be ashamed," I say. "If she'd come to me and told me all this, I would have been there for her."

"She said it was safer for you if you didn't know."

Safer? I'm struggling to understand just how dire the situation must have been. Not only did she not tell me about her relationship and pregnancy, but she was content with walking away from our entire life. Why? To try and protect me?

"How am I supposed to believe you about any of this?"

Adam shrugs. "I don't know. But it's the truth. The only reason I didn't say anything before is because I believed that's what Erin wanted. I never seriously worried the police would do anything to me, because there was never any foul play. At least, not from me. I figured whenever Erin was ready, she'd reach out to you.

"Now that the baby is here, I'm not so sure. She was adamant about being a mother. She wouldn't have given birth and just left her on your doorstep. I'm worried."

"Worried about what?"

"Maybe whoever she was running away from found her?"

I think of the phone call our mother received several months ago. Was that Erin's attempt to escape? Is it proof she's been held against her will all this time?

Then I consider Beth's theory. That Erin left willingly. Maybe Adam's story checks out, and once Erin was on her own in a different state, she decided to start a new life. Maybe she was happy leaving me and her friends and her career behind.

But what about Rosie?

Is it possible after the honeymoon period of parenting ended, she was fed up? Realized she couldn't raise a child, let alone on her own? And she couldn't come back to town and explain everything that happened for fear I wouldn't forgive her.

"Emily?" Adam's voice wakes me from my trance. "Are you okay? I know this is a lot to take in."

"I don't know what to think," I say, wobbling as I try to stand. Adam offers me his hand, but I brush him off.

"There were so many times I wanted to tell you the truth. It's always been clear to me how much you love your sister." He pauses. "But Erin insisted you were better off not knowing, and I wanted to keep my promise to her."

"This doesn't bring me any closer to answers," I say. If anything, all it presents are more questions.

"I really did love your sister," he says, calling after me after I start to walk away. "That's why I was willing to do whatever it took to protect her."

# TWENTY-FOUR

## ERIN

The Night of the Disappearance

The bench is uncomfortable, the wood damp and warped after so many years of exposure. At night, the train station is almost empty. We planned it this way. I don't hear many people talk about taking the train, and I thought it would be the ideal way to leave town unseen. A few weary travelers are within sight, but everyone seems locked inside their own little bubble, staring ahead at phones or at the suitcases beside them.

I'm confident no one is paying attention to me.

I've gone back to the ticket booth twice. Apparently, there's been a delay to the train's arrival time.

Only five more minutes, according to the new estimated time. It's the in between that's the most difficult. The waiting.

I close my eyes, inhaling the damp air around me.

"There you are," he says, the voice catching me off guard.

I'm ashamed to say it, but the first feeling I have is gratitude. He came back for me. I claim to want to start over—break away from him and everything else in my life—but it's romantic to be chased.

"What are you doing here?" I say. I need to stay focused, remember why I'm here.

"I realized I have to stop you." He sits beside me, the scent of his cologne tantalizing. We're not even touching and yet having him close to me seems to cut through the cold night air, his body heat swirling with mine. "It doesn't have to be this way."

"Yes, it does," I tell him, the excitement of the moment decreasing as reality sets in. "And you know it. We've already talked about it."

He shakes his head, and I'm again smitten with every detail. His smile and his strength and his caring. I've always prided myself on being an independent woman, but one glimpse of him and I want to melt into his arms.

"I don't know how I can carry on without you," he says. "I just want you to hear me out. Fully. Will you come with me for a drive?"

I look down at the empty tracks, wishing everything wasn't coming down to this one decision. "The train was supposed to be here thirty minutes ago."

"Maybe that's fate, then." His eyes are hopeful. "Don't you always say things happen for a reason?"

I used to say that. I used to think our relationship was some kind of fate or kismet. Whenever I think of all the other people we are hurting, my chest aches with regret. It was selfish of me to start this up, selfish of both of us. The only way to make things right again is for me to leave.

"There will be another train," he says, inching closer to me. "Just listen to what I have to say, and if you still want to go through with it, I'll never bother you again. I can't live with myself without telling you everything I'm feeling."

There's a dull ache in my stomach at the thought my actions might be causing him pain. I'm used to it being the other way around. "Feeling about what?"

"About you," he says. "And our future."

That one little word is what gets me every time. Future. The possibility that our story doesn't end here, on a cold, rainy night in some isolated train station. If he truly didn't care, wouldn't it be easier to let me go?

The fact that he's here proves he still loves me. I at least owe him the opportunity to express himself.

"Start talking," I say.

"Not here," he says, looking around the train station. It appears as abandoned now as it did earlier. There's a man in a coat and hat a few benches down. A couple across from him. I look at them and wonder about their lives, where they're going. What brought them here on this rainy night?

"Erin, please," he says. I see tears in his eyes. This isn't just about me, I realize. This is his choice to make, too. Our future. "Let's just take a ride."

Before I can answer, the train comes sweeping into the station. The passing wind blows back my hair, sends the lapels of my jacket flying. After so many minutes of cursing and waiting for its arrival, I'm not ready for it to be here. I'm not ready to make this decision.

I stand, my knees wobbling as I decide what direction to take. I could move forward, leave him behind and follow through with my decision. Or I could hear him out. Give him just one more chance to make it right. Give him the chance to choose me.

We don't say anything else for several minutes. Not until the train has boarded its passengers and left the station. I can see him trying to hide his smile about the fact we've been gifted a few more moments together.

"Thank you," he says.

"You owe me a train ticket," I say, as I walk toward the parking lot. I can feel his gaze on me.

"I owe you a lot more than that," he says, wrapping his arm

around my waist. I'm ashamed to admit how good it feels. Before exiting the station, I take one more glimpse at the schedule. The next train is early tomorrow morning. If I still want to go through with my decision, I can come back. A choice hasn't been made, just delayed.

We approach his car, the rain ceasing. I look up at the bright moon in the sky above us and wonder, did I make the right choice?

# TWENTY-FIVE
## EMILY

Hot tears sting my eyes as I march toward the car. I can feel Adam watching me, and I wonder what he's thinking. I wonder how much I should trust him.

Everything he's told me sounds impossible. For a year, I've blamed him for Erin's disappearance. I believed he murdered her.

Now, he's insisting he was only trying to help my sister. He claims Erin knew about her pregnancy and was in trouble. That she had no one to turn to.

What about me? I struggle to believe anything he says because I can't imagine a world where Erin wouldn't come to me. We've always supported each other, from the time we were children. If she had a new boyfriend, even one she thought I wouldn't approve of, she'd tell me about it. If she were pregnant, she'd tell me.

I've reckoned with the possibility that my judgements put a wedge between us, made her feel as though she had to keep secrets, but she can't think I'd judge her that harshly, could she? Why on earth would she avoid me in favor of Adam, her controlling and obsessive ex? Am I really supposed to believe she'd choose his help over mine?

And yet, I can't deny the fact that Adam appeared genuinely distraught when the conversation turned to Rosie. Any time we've communicated before, he's approached me with a defensive, even conceited, demeanor. Everything changed with the arrival of the baby. He seemed genuinely shocked and confused about why Erin would have left Rosie behind, and the DNA test proves he isn't the father, which further strengthens his claim that Erin was dating someone else at the time she went missing.

I think back to what Beth said about Erin willingly walking away. At the time, the idea angered me. Now, I've encountered two people in her life who are saying the same thing, and there's no denying that something was going on in Erin's life, something she didn't want me to know about. I didn't even know she'd reconnected with David. Everything I've uncovered suggests that, and upsettingly, connects to Adam's story, too.

Erin was asking for time off work, seemingly so she could leave town. She was behind on bills, putting her money toward her new life. Adam could still be lying, could still be involved in her death, but he's certainly putting a lot of effort into making sure his story aligns with what I've learned about Erin thus far. He may not be Rosie's father, but that doesn't mean he didn't harm Erin.

The drive back to my house passes in a flash, my thoughts trapped in a whirlwind of possibilities and confusion. This image of Erin that's being presented to me is at odds with the sister I know, the sister I love.

As I approach the front door, I look through the window to the left and catch a glimpse of Viv and Rosie. She's standing in the living room, shifting her weight from side to side, in what appears to be an attempt to soothe the baby. It's a touching moment.

It makes me wonder how different my life could have been if Erin had never gone missing. Maybe Byron and I would still be together. Maybe we'd have children, as planned. Viv could be here visiting my child instead of babysitting my niece in the middle of a crisis.

If Adam is telling the truth, and Erin knew she was pregnant before she went missing, it gives more depth to Beth's theory. Is it possible that Erin thought she could handle everything on her own, and when she realized she couldn't, she was the one who left Rosie on my doorstep? I imagine my long-lost sister waiting behind the bushes, watching me in the darkness, refusing to come forward, to offer an explanation.

The possibility fills me with anger. I can't imagine Erin being that selfish and irresponsible. Then again, I can't imagine her doing the other things people are saying she did either.

I walk inside, the air conditioner making my arm hairs stand at attention. Viv looks at me and smiles.

"She just woke up from a nap," she says, returning her focus to the baby.

"Was she easy?" I ask, trying to force some joy into my voice.

"A little angel. She napped most of the time." She moves closer to me, and I think she's going to hand her over, but she continues to cradle Rosie in her arms, as though she doesn't want to let her go. "What did you find out?"

"Nothing much," I say, sitting on the sofa. I never told Viv where I was really going, and I don't have the energy to unpack my conversation with Adam just yet. I need to try and make sense of it in my own mind. "I really appreciate you watching her."

"Anytime. I mean that," she says. She sits beside me, rolling Rosie out of her arms and into mine. "What are your plans for the rest of the day?"

I stare at Rosie, her large eyes framed with dark lashes. She raises her knuckles to her mouth and begins sucking on her own thumb.

"I don't know," I say. "Honestly, I have no idea what will happen from one day to the next."

Viv places her hand on my shoulder. "You don't have to figure out everything in one day."

I nod, knowing she's right. And yet, Viv doesn't understand the dilemma Rosie presents. She's never had a sister.

"I'll feel better once I know if Erin's okay," I admit.

Viv's body language closes up, and she looks as though she's debating what to say next.

"My advice? You need to focus on what's best for you and the baby." She looks at Rosie. "She's the one who needs you now."

She's right. Rosie is vulnerable and alone. The only thing stopping her from entering state care and a world of strangers is me. And yet, I can't switch my allegiance from Erin to Rosie that quickly. I've spent my entire life looking after Erin. If I'd kept searching for her instead of assuming she was dead, I might have been able to help sooner. There has to be a way I can bring Erin back to Rosie, where she belongs. Make things right.

Viv stands, as though she's afraid she's overstepped a boundary. "Matt needs me back at the office," she says, "but I can always tell him to screw off if you want me to stay."

"Go. I'll be fine," I say.

"Are you sure?"

I nod. Viv squeezes my shoulder and then gives Rosie a little wave. As helpful as she's been over the past couple of days, I wonder if there isn't a part of her that's relieved to be leaving. She has the chance to escape the madness that's consuming my life.

Rosie begins wiggling in my arms, a sure sign that she's

hungry. I go into the kitchen and prepare a bottle. She takes it gladly, her eyelids fluttering closed as she sucks in the chalky liquid.

Once she's settled, I take out my phone and call Detective Carson. I need to share Adam's story with him to see what he makes of it.

# TWENTY-SIX

Part of me dreads talking to Detective Carson. There's a possibility that my choice to seek out Adam on my own could backfire completely. He's already warned me to stay away from him, even went so far as to threaten me about taking Rosie away.

To his credit, when I get him on the line, he listens intently. I can hear a pen scratch against paper as he takes notes, and every so often, he curses under his breath.

"This information would have been helpful a year ago," he says.

"Adam insists he was only helping Erin," I say. "If we can believe what he says."

After all this time, it's not in my nature to take what Adam says as gospel. Even if Rosie isn't his biological child, there could still be reasons for him to hurt Erin.

"There's something else I've been meaning to tell you," I say, diving into the conversation I had with my mother. After the confrontations at the police station and the shock of the DNA test results, I'd overlooked this detail, but it could still be important. "My mother received a phone call from Erin months ago and never reported it. Is there any way to trace the call?" I ask, hopeful our only concrete lead isn't a dead end.

"We can try sifting through her phone records," he says, "but it will be difficult. Especially if we don't have an exact time and date."

I exhale in frustration. "I don't know why she didn't report it right away."

"If it's any consolation, we might not have been able to track anything down even if she had reached out."

I'm still upset by my mother's inaction. It's bad enough she wasn't an involved parent when we were younger, but even in adulthood, we can't depend on her.

"What about Adam?" I ask. "Are you going to talk to him again?"

"Definitely," he says, his voice skeptical. "It's hard to believe he was able to keep this secret for so long. If he's telling the truth about helping Erin leave of her own volition, he's been obstructing a police investigation."

I'm relieved to hear Detective Carson is as unsure of Adam as I am. If anything, he seems to feel Adam's new story makes him even more suspicious.

"You'll let me know after you talk to him?" I ask.

"I promise to follow up leads as they come in," he says.

"Does that mean you still haven't received the results of David's DNA test?" I'd been hoping he'd mention them.

He sighs. "Still nothing from the lab." I can't tell if he's being honest.

My hope deflates. I want to be involved with Erin's case. Remaining on the outskirts of the investigation is torture.

"Look, I know the past week has been intense, and I think it's really admirable you're willing to step up and take care of your sister's baby," he says. "It's a tough job to take on, especially by yourself. Lean on as many people as you need to help you care for the baby, and leave Erin's case to us, okay?"

I end the call, unsure how today's revelations make me feel. Adam's guilt is appearing less and less likely, and the fact David's DNA results haven't come in means I can't scratch him off the list. I'd never really considered him a suspect before, but the more I think about it, he sounds like the type of person Adam said Erin was trying to get away from. Maybe I need to shift my suspicions from Adam to him.

I consider reaching out to Marco at the paper. I've avoided giving him any information about Rosie and her relationship to Erin; even though I trust him not to run the story, it would put him in a difficult position. It's certainly salacious, and once people at the paper catch wind, there's no way they'll keep the story under wraps. Still, his resources are more far-reaching than mine. He could access more information about David.

I take out my phone and send him a message.

*Care to look into a possible suspect for me? It's about Erin.*

I'm relieved when a few minutes later, I get a response.

*Always. What's the name?*

If Marco had heard that Rosie was related to Erin, he would have surely asked more questions. I can't help feeling keeping her existence a secret is for the best right now. It allows me to focus on finding Erin and keeps Rosie safe.

I send over the limited information I have. David's full name and last known city of residence. I explain he's a former boyfriend of Erin's without going into the drama of their relationship. If Marco digs deep enough, I'm sure he'll find out, but I don't want anything to color his investigation. My research has shown that David is nothing more than a husband and family man, but, of course, looks can be deceiving. If Erin rekindled her relationship with him and he felt threatened by the pregnancy, it would certainly put her in a dangerous position.

One thing is for sure, I can't focus on finding Erin and taking care of Rosie by myself. I need to talk over everything with someone who is as invested in the case as I am. I need help. Reluctantly, I call Byron. He answers on the second ring.

"Have any dinner plans?" I ask him.

He almost sounds too cheerful when he responds. "I'll snag a table for three."

\* \* \*

When Byron's brother accepted a temporary job across the country he didn't want to lug all his belongings with him, so he decided to keep his apartment. That's come in handy in the wake of our separation. Just recently, Byron took over the lease, after it had sat empty for more than a year.

The apartment is only a few blocks away from our favorite Thai restaurant. I meet Byron there, after another tug of war between me and the car seat. There's already an order of steamed dumplings waiting on the table when I arrive.

Byron smiles when he catches a glimpse of Rosie, wide-awake in her carrier. For a moment, I feel like I've been transported to another dimension, a different life where Byron and I are still together, and we have a child of our own.

Everything with Rosie has come so easy to him. He's a natural. Somehow, I always knew this about him, and it's why I insisted on the divorce. Byron has always wanted to be a father, and I couldn't take that opportunity away from him. At the same time, the devastation I felt over Erin's disappearance was profound. It changed my view of the world and what I wanted from it. I don't know if I'll ever willingly have a child, knowing all the danger and uncertainty that exists.

I look at Rosie, her carrier in a sling at the end of our table, realizing all the worry and anxiety I'd been trying to avoid with my own child has now been transferred to her.

"I can't believe Adam isn't the baby's father," he says, balancing a wad of noodles between two chopsticks. "And I can't believe Viv let you talk to him on your own."

"I wasn't exactly truthful about what I was doing," I say. "She'd have warned me against it."

"I understand how invested you are, but you have to leave the investigating to the police," he says. "If something happens to you, that won't bring us any closer to finding out what happened to Erin." He pauses. "So, what do you think now?"

"I don't know," I say, reluctant to speak my own thoughts into existence. "I've always thought Adam was at the center of it all. And I guess I was right, in a sense. If everything he said about helping her escape this new boyfriend is true, he was trying to help her."

Byron shakes his head. "I've never seen two sisters as close as you were," he says. "If she were in trouble, she would have come to you, not her ex."

"That's what worries me," I say. "What if Erin did decide to walk away from her life? That's what Beth suggested. And now Adam, too. She'd come to me if she were in trouble, but not if she wanted to escape."

"You would have talked her out of going."

"Exactly." I take a sip of my drink, my fingers damp with condensation. "It makes me wonder if she was trying to get away. If she thought she could somehow handle being a parent on her own, and when she realized it was too hard, she brought Rosie back."

To my left, Rosie's feet dance in the air, her little arms stretching to reach her toes. There's a bittersweet feeling coming over me, a mix of relief and resentment. Byron stares at the baby, too.

"I can't imagine Erin doing that," he says. "Abandoning her own child."

That's what concerns me the most about everything we've uncovered over the past few days. It makes me wonder if I've ever known my sister at all.

"If Adam isn't the father, there must have been someone else in her life," I say, thinking back to my other confrontation at the police station. "Maybe the police are right and I have to consider other suspects. Like David."

"Who is David?"

I sigh. Even though I need to fill Byron in on all the details, it feels wrong talking about Erin's past. "When she was in college, there was some drama with an ex-boyfriend."

"How so?"

"David was a TA in her creative writing class. Erin started dating him when she was still a student, and the school wasn't happy about it."

"How old was she?"

"Early twenties. He couldn't have been thirty. It wasn't the age difference as much as the abuse of power. The university had a zero-tolerance policy when it came to students and staff, as they should."

"So, what happened?"

"Rumors started to spread. The school found out about the relationship, and David was fired," I say. "As expected, they broke up soon after that. Erin tried to keep the whole thing hushed up, but eventually I found out."

"And you think this David guy might be involved with what's happening now?"

"I didn't at first. But when I showed up at the police station to see Adam, David was there, too. Police had reached out to him and asked him to submit a DNA test."

Byron looks confused. "Just because he was an ex?"

"They'd been messaging each other back and forth on social

media." I shake my head. "If they started their relationship back up, she wouldn't have wanted to tell me about it."

"Was the guy controlling? Dangerous?"

"Not that I knew back then," I say. "But he's married now. And has two young kids. I looked him up online. If he had an affair with Erin and she got pregnant, it could have sent him off the deep end. He wouldn't want the same woman ruining his life twice."

Byron nods, thinking.

The waitress comes over to our table and I ask for a takeout box.

Byron already has his card out. "One check," he says, before she can bring over the bill.

I thank him, grateful for his kindness in the wake of everything that's happened, but I can't shake this paranoid feeling inside. Why did Erin feel the need to keep so many secrets from me? And could one of those secrets be responsible for what happened to her?

# TWENTY-SEVEN

## ERIN

The Night of the Disappearance

We were supposed to talk, but for most of the drive, we stay silent. Everything I'm feeling sits on the tip of my tongue, but I'm not brave enough to let it out.

Was I ever brave enough, I wonder? Did I really think I could sneak away from my life undetected? No, I knew my life would change forever. I think that's the real reason I decided to leave the train station. I want to cling to my former life just a little bit longer.

Soon, the road turns familiar, the foliage on the branches overhead banding together in a thick canopy. He's taking me to our special place.

He raises his head, my whole body tingling at the sight of his smile. "Are you okay with this?"

I nod, but don't say anything else. We've come here many times before. It's the only place that feels like an escape. Right now, it's too dark to see, but I only need to close my eyes and imagine the landscape around me. Imagine the roaring fireplace and comfortable bed inside.

The rain picks back up before we're able to park, so we hurry out of the car and rush inside. As quick as we are, I'm still drenched, my clothes clinging to my flesh, chill bumps spreading across my arms and torso. Instinctively, he pulls me closer, trying to warm me. His bare hands soak up the moisture, replacing the cold with warmth, then land on my stomach.

"What were you planning to do, Erin?"

It's painful having to say the words out loud, but I must.

"We can't be together," I say. "Let alone raise a child."

"We've barely even had time to talk about this."

"Time isn't on our side," I say. I didn't find out about the baby until a few weeks ago. I've never been good at keeping up with my cycle. It's been erratic since I was a teenager. I'm still in the first trimester, but the baby will be here before we know it.

"And you plan on raising this child by yourself?" he asks. "Being a single parent?"

"I can do this," I say, confident. "A baby will only complicate your life. But me? This could be what I need. Maybe it's time I start caring for someone besides myself."

He goes to the fireplace. He throws a few logs on and lights a match. In silence, I watch as the flames rise and flicker, spreading warmth throughout the room. I move closer, the heat from the flames warming my cheeks, making them rosy.

"Maybe there's another way," he says.

"Another way for what?"

He looks at me, his face still, as though he's as afraid of what he's about to say as I am to hear it. "We could be together."

I look into my lap. It's cruel to tempt me with this after all this time. Our entire relationship has been a secret, a shame. How is the pregnancy, our baby, to be any different?

"No, we can't."

"Erin, I've loved you for longer than I want to admit. Before you came into my life, I'd just been going through the motions. Pretending to be happy. With you and the baby," he says, pausing to look at my growing stomach, "I might have a real chance."

"What about your life—"

"*You* are my life now." He comes closer, placing his hands on my cheeks. The way he cradles my head so tenderly makes me want to smile and cry all at once. "This is what I want."

"How would we ever make it work?"

"We can start over together." He looks around the room. "Here, if you like. You've always loved this place."

I laugh. "You're just going to walk away from everything and move here?"

"We could. Or we could go somewhere else together."

It feels as though he's snuck into some secret part of me and stolen my deepest desires. How many times have I thought about running away together? I've had lazy weekends here that I never wanted to end. I imagined a different world, just the two of us, away from all the stressors of life. It was always a fantasy, nothing more, but now he's trying to make it a reality.

"Don't tell me what you think I want to hear," I say.

"I'm telling you it because it's true," he says. "We can do this together, if that's what you want."

I look at my stomach. From the moment I found out I was pregnant, I've been thinking of all the negative repercussions. I imagined the difficulties of being a single parent, something I'd witnessed firsthand with my own mother. I didn't want to put myself, or this child, through that.

Even worse, I dread how Emily will react when the truth comes out. Having this baby means hurting the person who loves me the most, maybe even losing her altogether. When I think about Emily finally learning the truth, imagining the disbelief in her pained expression, I want nothing more than to disappear. My chest becomes unbearably heavy, weighed down with regret and shame.

And yet, I've never taken the time to consider what it would be like to raise a child with him. For the fantasy future in my mind and the reality of my present to merge, the three of us against the world, becoming a happy family. Sure, there would be casualties. We'd lose people that were important along the way, but what would we gain? Each other? Happiness? Freedom?

I think of what it would be like to be a mother, to raise a little boy or little girl with a devoted partner by my side. I could provide this child with all the things I never had. Without realizing it, a tear trails down my cheek. When I look up at him, he's smiling.

"All I need is some time to get my affairs in order," he says. "You can stay here. Rest and relax. I've already put too much stress on you and our baby."

*Our baby.* Amazing how one conversation can change our entire lives.

"You can stay here as long as you like."

"Will you stay with me?" I ask.

"Of course I will," he says. "At least for tonight."

# TWENTY-EIGHT

## EMILY

As I'm lifting Rosie's carrier into the back seat of my car, I catch a whiff of something rancid.

"Oh no. She might have had an accident," I say. I move the blanket covering her legs. Sure enough, there's a nasty mess spilling out the sides of her diaper. I gag, as the pungent smell overwhelms my senses. "I think I'm going to be sick."

"You want me to change her?" Byron asks.

"She needs a whole new outfit," I say, looking at the diaper bag, feeling completely underprepared. I've never dealt with a mess of this magnitude. "I didn't bring any extra clothes."

"I've picked up a few things I meant to give you," he says, nodding in the direction of his apartment. "Come inside, and you can get her cleaned up."

I look between my car and the sidewalk, trying to decide. I don't want to leave Rosie sitting in her own filth. Even if I did, I'm not sure I could stand the short car ride back to the house with that smell. Reluctantly, I unhook the carrier and start following Byron down the sidewalk. His place is only a block ahead. When we reach the concrete steps leading to his building, he takes the carrier from my hands.

"Let me help," he says.

I don't argue with him. My shoulder is already stinging from the extra weight of lugging Rosie around.

He holds the carrier with one hand, using his other to unlock the front door. We walk inside, and a wave of sadness comes over me. The apartment itself isn't dilapidated or small, but it's a far cry from the home we once shared together. There's a mix of other furniture, some familiar, some new. The place reminds me of the first apartment he had when we started dating back in college.

"It would be easier to change her in the bedroom," he says, pointing down the lone hallway. "Or I can do it."

"It's fine," I say, unfastening the buckles across Rosie's chest. I lift her cautiously, holding her tiny body out in front of me, trying to avoid the mess.

When Erin was born, I'd change her diapers all the time, but I don't remember the task seeming so disgusting. I think I've been set in my ways for too long. Back then, the promise of a baby sister was so rewarding, even a nasty diaper couldn't turn me off the idea. Also, I knew, even then, that our own mother had problems. Erin needed me, and that sense of responsibility outweighed any potential disgust.

I enter Byron's bedroom to find it's as dressed down as the rest of the apartment. Nothing personal on the walls or night-stand. It's clear this is only a bridge between places, and it saddens me how lonely that is for both of us.

Rosie starts squirming more as I put her on the bed. "It's okay," I soothe her, pulling out the necessary materials from the diaper bag.

It takes longer to clean her up than usual. Part of me wishes I could just throw her in the bath, but that would be too much of an intrusion. It's weird being in a place that is Byron's and not mine. It's weird that I'm here at all right now, my missing sister's baby the only link left between us.

Before going back out into the hallway, I take one more look around the sad little room. I wonder if he's brought a woman back here, if he's dating at all. It's been the furthest thing from my mind, even before Rosie showed up. Choosing to move forward with the divorce was accepting the fact Byron could have the family he always wanted, just not with me. I close the door behind me, trying to think of anything else.

Byron is waiting. "Want me to dig out some clothes?"

"Sure," I say, handing Rosie over. "I was going to wash up first."

"Of course," he says, carrying Rosie with him to the living room.

I scrub my hands until my skin feels raw but I still get the lingering whiff of a dirty diaper. It's tremendous how much my life has changed in a few short days. I wonder, with a shudder, if this is how Erin felt, if it's the reason she decided to leave Rosie behind. Maybe it was all harder than she realized.

Outside the bathroom, I can hear Byron singing "Itsy Bitsy Spider" to Rosie in the living room. I shake my head and smile. As difficult as parenting can be for some people, and I certainly assign myself to that camp, it comes naturally for others. It comes naturally for him.

I notice another door cracked open beside the bathroom. Curiosity gets the best of me, and I peek inside, wondering what Byron has done with the second bedroom of his sad little apartment.

There's no bed in sight. He's fitted this room out as his office, as I should have expected. In our own house, Byron's only requirement had been a quiet room where he could work. That later extended into a man cave in the garage and a shed in the backyard. Byron's always put work first. It's something that attracted me to him in the first place.

My eyes wander away from the desk with its lone lamp. Across from it, I see a baby swing and a bassinet. This must be what he was telling me about, the things he bought to give me, even though I already have a bassinet at my own house. Why would he purchase a second one? I wonder if he scoured the internet looking for a good secondhand deal, or if he purchased these items brand new.

I walk inside the room, feeling the plush fabric along the edges of the bassinet, the material a light-green gingham. As usual, Byron is doing too much, and yet, part of me wonders how I would have made it through any of this without him.

I turn to leave the way I came when something catches my eye. Erin. A large picture of her is tacked on the center of the wall behind me. Her smile hypnotizes me, drawing me closer, and yet it's surprising seeing her here, in this dowdy apartment with no personality or style. Why does Byron have a picture of her on the wall?

That's when I take in the other materials surrounding the picture. There are newspaper clippings, all the major headlines from when Erin first went missing. And besides that, there's more. Index cards with different details about her life. Where she worked. Her height and weight. Notes about the various people in her life. There's even a note about David, the teaching assistant I mentioned to Byron over dinner. The entire time I told him the story, he acted as though he knew nothing about it. Now I see he's unpacked every detail of my sister's life and memorialized it on his office wall.

I take a step back, the many pictures of Erin staring back at me, a collage of my missing sister. Open cardboard boxes sit on the floor beneath the display. I bend down and begin sifting through them, finding half-used journals and fairy lights and concert posters. A lilac bedspread.

These are Erin's belongings from her apartment, not just research that could be pulled from the internet. How did Byron get them?

I feel as though I'm going to be sick.

"Emily? Are you back here?" Byron's voice carries down the hallway. He's getting close, too close for me to somehow exit the room without him seeing me.

He pushes open the door, Rosie still in his hands, his expression dropping when he sees the look on my face.

"What the hell is this?" I ask him, pointing at the wall.

Byron looks as though he's been caught doing something wrong.

"I can explain—"

"You have dozens of pictures of Erin and notes about her life," I say, thinking of all the times he'd encouraged me to back away from her case. Move on. "You're obsessed."

"I'm not obsessed," he says. "You're taking this the wrong way."

"She's my missing sister, Byron. How am I supposed to take it?" My eyes land on Rosie. I step closer to them. "Give me the baby."

He hesitates, only for a moment, before handing her over. "Let me explain."

"I don't want to talk anymore," I say, feeling desperate to get out of this apartment, the sad, drab walls feeling as though they're about to collapse in on me.

"Emily, please."

I ignore him, stomping past him and into the living room. I place Rosie in the car seat, strapping her in as fast as I can. Miraculously, I fasten her in quickly, and I heave the carrier out the front door.

"Emily, don't leave like this," Byron says, following me to the door. "You're upset."

I ignore him, stumbling down the cement stairs, almost losing my balance before I reach the sidewalk. For a brief moment, I'm afraid Rosie and her carrier will go tumbling out of my arms.

Of course, I'm upset, but it's more than that. I've just discovered that my soon-to-be ex-husband is obsessed with my missing sister. Every day, it seems, I lose another person I thought I could trust.

# TWENTY-NINE

I barely sleep, but this time, I can't blame it on Rosie. After downing a full bottle of formula, she slept soundly, making little cooing sounds throughout the night. I sat up in my bed, unable to sleep, thinking about Erin and Byron.

It was unsettling seeing so many pictures of my sister inside my ex-husband's apartment.

Byron has known Erin almost as long as he's known me, and she was a regular fixture in our home, in our lives. He was just as devastated by her disappearance as I was. As the days turned into weeks, he talked about her less and less, but I thought that was on account of me. Every time her name was mentioned, I'd lash out.

When it became clear my grief over losing my sister was tearing us apart, she became the constant elephant in the room, the wedge between us. I knew there was nothing that could replace her, and all he could do was let me revel in my grief. We reached a point where we quit talking about her completely. She became a ghost. When I did get too involved, he'd become angry with me.

Now, I see he's been obsessed with her disappearance.

Tracking everything he can about her in the media, even going so far as to investigate her past. Why wouldn't he tell me any of this? And when did this obsession start? He certainly didn't have any of that stuff when he was still living in the house. It's as though the moment he moved into the apartment he started obsessing over my dead sister.

My *not* dead sister, I remember. Rosie proves that. Or at least she proves Erin was alive the better part of this year. I wonder if, in his manic research, Byron has uncovered any new information. If he had, wouldn't he have told me?

Another thought enters my mind, this one darker.

Adam insisted Erin was in a relationship with someone she couldn't tell me about. Is it possible that person was Byron? The idea of my husband and sister together makes me sick; I can't imagine either of them betraying me like that. And yet, isn't that the precise scenario you see splashed across true crime dramas and television series? An unthinkable situation spiraling into something even more dangerous and wicked.

Is it possible that's why Byron had all those pictures? A shrine to my sister. And I can't ignore the fact he had a ton of baby stuff. The space lacks all personal mementos but is filled with baby supplies. And he's such a natural with Rosie. As though, maybe, he's been around her before.

My thoughts whirl around my brain. I feel sick, insane. I've been going around in circles trying to figure out why Erin wouldn't confide in me. Maybe now I know why she couldn't tell me the truth. Because she knew it would destroy me. It would have to be something of that magnitude to keep her from telling me the truth, I'm sure of it.

I race into the bathroom, fearful I might vomit. I splash cold water onto my face, desperate for anything to stop this sickening feeling inside. I need a distraction from my own thoughts.

It's almost depressing that the only place I feel comfortable going is the office. I've always been someone who threw herself into work, even back at the newspaper. I'd obsess over leads and details and stories, making sure I got everything right.

My actual work isn't as exciting here, but working for my best friend makes up for it. This company was Viv's dream, and there's a rewarding feeling knowing I'm helping contribute, even a little bit.

Still, I don't realize how strange it is that I'm walking into my office with Rosie strapped to my chest. It doesn't hit me until I see the looks on people's faces. Their familiar smiles are soon swapped out for wide-eyed stares as they see Rosie. They all must be wondering the same thing. How did she get a baby?

The only person who isn't stunned by my arrival is Viv. She sees me through the glass walls leading to her office and stands. Matt, on the other hand, looks as bothered as the rest of our co-workers. "I had no idea you were coming," she says. "Or that you were bringing the baby."

"I couldn't be alone at the house anymore," I say. "And I didn't know where else to go."

Viv nods. "What about Byron?"

I only give her a look, showing how upset I am. "We're not speaking right now."

"What's wrong?"

"I don't even know where to start."

Viv takes Rosie while I prepare a bottle. Once the baby is settled, I dive into the details about my conversation with the police, explaining everything Adam told me.

"Why wouldn't you tell Viv the truth about where you were going?" Matt asks. "It was completely stupid for you to go there on your own."

Viv looks at me, a mix of concern and curiosity in her stare. "You shouldn't have lied to me."

"I didn't want to worry you," I say.

"Adam was always a creep," Viv says. "I can't imagine he was helping her this whole time."

"I don't think he was continuing to help her," I say. "He took her to the train station, but after that, he said they lost contact. He said she talked about some plan of starting over. That she dreamed of moving to some cabin near the woods and raising the baby on her own."

"So, he just let her go?" Viv says, her tone disbelieving.

"According to him, she sent him one message telling him she was safe, and that was it."

"If he's telling the truth," Matt adds.

I think, going through the same theories I've had before. "I'm having a friend do some more digging into David. We're still waiting on his test results."

"Unless there was someone else you didn't know about," Viv says. She says it cautiously, as though she's afraid I'll snap at her. "I mean, Adam's story does line up with what we already know. She had asked for days off work. And now we know why."

She looks at Rosie. It still doesn't make sense to me that Erin would want to start over on her own.

My phone begins to ring, Byron's name flashing across the screen. I silence the call but not before Viv catches the name.

"What's going on with the two of you?" she asks.

I skipped over the part about visiting his sad, little apartment and finding the shrine to my missing sister. The information about Adam felt more relevant.

"Don't worry about it," I say.

The words no sooner leave my lips than we're interrupted by a knock at the door. I look through the glass walls to see Steven standing on the other side. My stomach turns. I haven't seen him since I realized he's been living in Erin's old apartment.

"I thought that was you," he says, poking his head inside the room. He blanches when he sees the baby. "Whose is the kid?"

"Mine," I say, surprising myself with how quickly the response leaves my lips, my readiness to claim her as my own.

"I didn't know you had—"

"Can we help you, Steven?" Matt says, mercifully changing the subject.

Steven clears his throat. "I was just relieved to see Emily is back. I've been wanting to go over the plans for the Denver office since last week."

"Sure," I say, standing. Viv might be my best friend, but it's still humiliating being made to look like a slacker in front of my boss.

Viv raises her hand, commanding me to sit. "Emily is here to visit with me. She isn't working today."

Steven's cheeks flush, his eyes cutting over to me. "With all due respect, the new office is expected to open next month. We can't finalize any of the plans we've made without the head copywriter's input."

I turn to Viv. "I'm fine, really. There's no reason anything should get held back because of me."

Matt stands, marching to the door before I can. "I'll take a look at whatever you're worried about."

Steven cuts his eyes at me again, a look that says he's irritated.

"What is his problem?" I ask Viv, after he leaves the room.

"He's just trying to show he's taking his job seriously," she says. "He had big shoes to fill."

"No, you're right. Erin was great at her job. If she were still here the second office would probably be open by now." Still, something about Steven's presence doesn't sit right. "Did you know he moved into her apartment?"

"You're kidding," she says. "When did you find that out?"

"When I visited Beth this week. I can't believe I forgot to mention it."

It's even stranger that after our encounter in the apartment

Beth didn't tell Steven about the baby. He looked at Rosie like he was genuinely surprised to see her.

"That is a weird coincidence," Viv says. "What are the odds someone would take her job and her apartment?"

Viv's eyes drift down to Rosie. I wonder if she's thinking the same thing I am. That Rosie is all we have left of Erin. Everything else, it seems, has been replaced. Rosie's thick dark eyelashes flutter. Something warm begins to stir inside my chest. Is this what maternal instincts feel like? That I'm willing to do whatever it takes, no matter how uncomfortable, to keep her safe?

# THIRTY

## ERIN

Ten Days Missing

It's like being on an endless vacation.

The first week, he comes over as much as possible, always bringing me plenty of food and beverages and comforts. When he's away, I spend my days wandering around, basking in the calm and solitude. Once he returns, we spend our time eating and giggling and making love.

We've decided on baby names. Madilynn for a girl, Bennett for a boy. Right now, I can't sense what the child might be, only that the morning sickness seems to grow every day. Still, it doesn't matter. Not when I'm here, with him.

I hadn't realized until I came here just how much I was sacrificing in my old life, just how unhappy I was. For months, I've been beating myself up for this relationship, hating myself for making such a stupid mistake again. Now, I see that this was meant to be. Maybe our love needs a different environment in order to thrive. It didn't originate in the best of circumstances, but something beautiful is coming out of it. Our baby.

As much as the escape has been fun, I do miss parts of my old life. More than anything, I miss Emily.

Choosing a life with him means I'll have to forfeit my relationship with her. There's no way she'll ever forgive me for what I've done. She'll be angry and ashamed of me. I'd found myself in yet another messy situation. I imagine Emily's outraged tone, her pained expression when she learns the truth.

For that reason, maybe the distance between us is a good thing. It provides perspective. I'd thought I needed to start over completely if I wanted to escape the shame of my situation. There's no doubt Emily will be angry with my choices, hurt that I didn't come to her before taking off, but maybe if I reach out to her and try to explain myself, we can build a path toward forgiveness.

The next night, he arrives for dinner. He's gotten takeout from one of our favorite spots in the city, and I'm reminded again of how wonderful it is having my every desire at my fingertips, after what feels like having to withhold my true needs for so long. As much as I want to continue living in this fantasy, I must start trying to repair my relationship with my sister.

"I need to talk to Emily," I tell him.

He's raising the fork to his mouth, noodles wrapped around the tongs. At first, I wonder if he's heard me. He chews in silence, calculating his response.

"Are you sure?" he says, at last. "I thought you were afraid of how she would react."

"I was." I am, if I'm being honest. I've withstood Emily's wrath before, but cutting her out of my life, trying to start over without her, isn't the answer. I see that now. "I know she's going to be furious." I look down, rub a hand over my stomach. "Maybe, in time, she can find a way to forgive me."

He nods, sipping his water. He's stopped drinking alcohol as yet another way to support me during the pregnancy. I love how we're tackling every stage of this process together. I wish Emily could see this, how the baby has brought out the best in both of us.

"Of course, she will," he says. "I know how close the two of you are."

That comment stings, even though I'm sure that wasn't his intention. We have always been close. Emily and I share every aspect of our lives with one another.

Except for this. I know she'll be hurt by my choices, but if anyone is capable of forgiving me, it's her.

"She must be wondering where I am," I say. "Going a few days without talking is one thing, especially after our fight at the restaurant. It's been over a week now."

"We agreed staying out of town was the best for the time being."

He's right. Truth is, I don't want to go back home. That seems like going backwards, slipping into an old skin. Screw my apartment and my job and the people I considered my friends.

I belong here, where I can focus on the new life we're building together. Our family. The only thing missing is Emily.

"My phone is dead," I say, even though he's already aware. "The internet connection isn't working, either."

"I know." He goes very still, thinking. "How about you write her a letter?"

"A letter?" I laugh, the idea seeming ridiculous. There's something old-fashioned about communicating that way in this modern world, but if being here has taught me anything, it's the importance of slowing down, the value of tradition. "That's not a bad idea. I can tell her not to worry about me."

"Are you going to tell her..." he pauses, looking for the right word "...everything?"

"Should I?" I lean forward, eager for his response. "I feel like I should tell her about the baby in person."

"Obviously, she'll find out eventually," he says. My heart

sinks at his next response. "I still need a little more time to get everything sorted."

He stands quickly, walking across the room to an old writing desk in the corner. He pulls out a drawer, taking out blank sheets of paper and a pen. Coming over to me, he bends down to kiss me on the cheek.

"Tell her anything you want," he says, "and I'll make sure she gets it."

The guilt I was feeling earlier weakens. I hope I can have everything I want from life. My relationship and my sister. Most importantly, my baby. I spend the rest of the night writing out all my feelings, trying to find the exact phrases to make Emily understand, to make her forgive me.

When he leaves the next morning, he takes the letter with him. For the next day, I lounge around, waiting. Sleeping is the only thing that seems to keep my nausea at bay, so even in the daytime, I keep the curtains drawn, reading old books and magazines to pass the time before he comes back.

When I hear his car in the drive, I jump in excitement, all but waiting for him at the door like an eager pet.

"Did you give her the letter?" I ask him. "Did she send anything back?"

Already, my stomach is in knots. I can tell by the look on his face that something is wrong. He's dreading our conversation.

"She read the letter," he says. "But it was too late."

"Too late?" I ask, confused.

"She found out about us," he says. "About everything."

My knees go weak as I stumble backward into the closest chair. I hadn't meant for Emily to go investigating on her own. I'd hoped I could tell her the worst part face to face, try and make her understand.

"How... how do you know?"

"She confronted me." I notice his red-rimmed eyes, his askew tie. "Told me she never wants to see either of us again."

It feels like I've been punched in the stomach. I'm unsure if it's another wave of morning sickness, or the dread over what he's telling me.

"She can't mean that," I say, my voice a whisper.

He shakes his head. "She's angry. She feels betrayed."

Avoiding those reactions are why I ran away in the first place. I didn't want to disappoint my sister, but I thought telling her the truth at the right time would help mend the situation. I never meant for her to figure things out on her own.

"Let's drive into town," I say, standing. "If she sees me in person, she'll calm down."

"I don't think so," he says, his voice shaking. "She called you a disappointment. A mistake." He pauses, struggling to get the next part out. "She said you'll end up no different than your mother."

My throat is raw with emotion, and yet I'm too stunned to cry. I can't imagine Emily saying those things, and yet, hadn't she brought up our mother the last time we were together?

Seeing the devastation on my face, he rushes over, putting his hands on either side of my face. "She's wrong. About everything. You're not going to end up like your mother because you won't be doing this alone. I'm here with you."

My heart bursts with gratitude, but it's a weakened sensation compared to everything else I'm feeling. Sadness. Loss. Shame. I cry, guttural sobs escaping from somewhere deep inside me.

"I never thought Emily would turn her back on me," I say, struggling to get the words out.

"You don't need her," he says, pressing his lips to my cheek. "We don't need anyone but each other."

# THIRTY-ONE

## EMILY

When I pull into my driveway, Byron's car fills my normal parking spot. He's sitting on the porch in one of the wooden rocking chairs we bought to commemorate our fifth wedding anniversary.

I can't muster the strength to confront him, so I sit in the driver's seat, staring.

Part of me thinks it's ridiculous to even consider Byron a suspect. He's my husband. The closest person to me besides Erin. If he were responsible for hurting her—killing her—it would upend everything I believe about my life.

And yet, if what Adam told me yesterday is true, something would have to be that huge in order for Erin to take off without confiding in me first. Whatever choices she was making, she felt ashamed. I can't imagine she'd sink so low as to sleep with Byron, but she wouldn't be the first person to make a colossal mistake. No one ever thinks the two people closest to them would betray them, but it happens.

Byron raises his head and stands. The movement signals me into action. I open the driver's side door, blocking him from approaching the back seat, where Rosie's car seat rests.

"What are you doing here?" I ask, raising my chin in defiance.

"You wouldn't answer my calls," he says, desperation tingeing every word.

"I have nothing to say to you."

"There's a lot I want to say," he says. "At least give me the opportunity to explain."

I lean against the car, arms crossed over my chest. "For months, you told me I'd gone overboard with this case. That I'm letting my obsession ruin everything in my life, our marriage included." My mind conjures the image of the photo-covered wall in his apartment. "Then I see your new bachelor pad is a miniature shrine to my sister. You've collected more information about her disappearance than I have."

"I'm a journalist, Emily," he says. "That's how I operate."

"Are you writing a piece about my sister?"

"Of course not," he says. "I'm only trying to figure out what happened to her."

"I had no idea you were looking into Erin's case."

"Why wouldn't I be? She was like a sister to me. Besides you and your mom, I'm the person who wants to know what happened to her the most."

"Then why wouldn't you tell me?"

"I didn't want to upset you."

Erin has certainly become a point of contention between us, but that's only because he thought I'd become obsessed. From the looks of his office, he's been the same.

"It must have taken you weeks to gather all that information. You already knew about David," I say, recalling the pictures of him Byron had plastered on the wall. "Why didn't you say anything?"

Byron shakes his head. "You'd never told me about it before. I learned about it when I was questioning some of her old classmates. I can't say I'm surprised it happened, but I was surprised you never told me."

It still feels wrong divulging all her secrets. The situation with David was, perhaps, her biggest mistake, one I thought she'd learned from.

"What do you mean it doesn't surprise you?"

"Erin has a way of getting herself in trouble," he says. "I say that from a victimology standpoint. No judgement."

It's easy to take immediate offense. There's a fine line between blaming the victims and analyzing their choices. Some areas of Erin's life were high-risk. She was young, in a controlling relationship and had an unpredictable schedule. Still, I can't understand why she wouldn't come to me with any problem she was in.

And I can't understand why Byron would keep me in the dark about what he was doing.

"But why? Why would you start digging after we decided to call it quits?"

He sighs again. "Because we both know her disappearance is what tore us apart. I thought if I could give you answers, I might be able to fix us."

The honesty of his response takes me by surprise. It feels like I've been hit hard in the chest. Erin wasn't my only heartbreak in the past year. I lost my marriage, too. Over the past few days, with the arrival of Rosie, he's been back in my life, and it's been nice. A comforting feeling. One that almost overwhelms the sadness of knowing our marriage is all but dead, the unsigned divorce papers still sitting in my house.

"We can still find out what happened to Erin," he says. "Get justice for her."

This is his chance to win me back, he thinks. Looking into Erin's disappearance is an opportunity for him to avoid the fact we're getting divorced. A distraction.

"You're not just investigating." My throat is raw with

emotion. "You have her things. Journals and personal belong-ings. Where did you get them?"

"Beth."

I recall our visit. She'd told me she'd boxed up Erin's stuff to make room for her new roommate. "Why would Beth give Erin's things to you?"

"Your relationship with her turned south," he says. "She didn't feel like she could come to you, but she didn't want to throw it all away. So, she came to me."

Another plausible explanation, but is it enough? If Byron has kept Erin in hiding for a year, that would make him a master manipulator. My love for him makes it too difficult to see the truth.

"What about all the baby supplies in your apartment?" I ask. "Where did you get them?"

"The local baby store," he says. "One of the workers helped me."

"Those things aren't cheap," I say, remembering the exorbi-tant cost of my own shopping spree.

"I figured you could end up having Rosie for the long haul. It's better to be prepared." Byron is always taking care of me. He looks at me with tears in his eyes. "Emily, I would never do anything to hurt your sister. You can't really think I'm involved, right?"

"I need space from everyone right now." I move to the left and open the back-seat passenger door to retrieve Rosie. I'm ready to get her inside and end this conversation. "Including you."

"What can I do to prove to you I'm telling the truth?"

My eyes fall on Rosie, a radical idea coming to mind. "You can give a DNA sample."

Byron takes a step back. "What?"

"The police already told me Adam isn't the father," I say.

"Whoever fathered this child is likely involved in Erin's disappearance."

"And you think that person is me?" His jaw clenches as he raises his hand to cover his face. He turns away from me entirely, facing the house, and I wonder if he's trying to temper his emotions or hide his reaction from me entirely. When he speaks, he sounds hurt, wounded. "I can't believe you'd ask me to do that."

"After everything that's happened in the past year—in the past week—I can't trust anyone. Either submit to a DNA test or give me space." Part of me feels like I'm betraying Byron in asking him to do this, but the past year has made me question everything. I can't let anyone—even him—have my complete trust. Rosie deserves protection from anyone who might be involved in her mother's disappearance.

I mount the stairs, cradling Rosie's carrier in both hands. Once I'm on the porch, I see a series of boxes on the other side of the rocking chairs. "What's this?"

Byron doesn't even lift his head. "It's the boxes Beth gave me. And everything else I've uncovered in my digging over the past year. I brought it for you."

"Why?"

"I'm trying to show you I'm only here to help," he says. "You can trust me."

The sheer amount of information is overwhelming. It's obvious Byron has done a thorough job of looking into the case. Then again, this could be another form of manipulation. A way for him to try and weasel back into my life.

As much as it hurts, I consider all the reasons he could be involved. On the night Rosie arrived on my doorstep, Byron showed up within an hour. He claimed he heard our address over the police scanner, but what if that's a lie? Maybe he's the one who left her behind. He's comfortable with Rosie, even more than I am. He gave her a name! There's a ton of baby supplies in his apartment, and even though he insists he bought everything for me, what if it was already there? He could have been bonding with Rosie for months, which explains the closeness between them. Explains the reasons he's so desperate to help me.

"I've told you what you need to do," I say, turning to face him. "Until you take a DNA test, there's nothing else to talk about."

# THIRTY-TWO

## ERIN

Twenty Days Missing

Ever since he told me about Emily's reaction, it's all I can think about.

I imagine how disappointed she is in me. I think of those horrible comments she made, wonder what she says about me to the other people in our lives.

Part of me can't blame her. If I were in her position, I might do the same thing. She must feel so upset, so ashamed. I only wish she'd give me the opportunity to fully explain myself. If I had the chance to talk to her in person, she'd forgive me. She must.

At least I have him.

He's been coming every other day, keeping the place stocked with everything I need. Clean clothes and fresh food. He even went to a local pharmacy to get more prenatal vitamins.

I only wish he didn't have to leave.

At first, he came to visit every night. He'd stay over most weekends. I knew he wouldn't be able to walk away in a mere day. Life is complicated, but as the days went on, it became harder to ignore that I was only a small part of his world. As happy as I was living our fantasy life together, he inevitably returned to the reality, and I had no idea what story was unfurling out there, especially now that Emily knew the truth. Had she forgiven him, even if she couldn't forgive me?

"I'm getting tired of being here alone," I say to him.

We've finished dinner. Takeout from one of my favorite restaurants, yet again, but this time it didn't taste so fantastic. It was stale and unseasoned. I'm not sure if my tastebuds are changing or if the allure of the endless vacation is wearing off.

"What are you talking about?" He flicks sudsy water off his fingers onto my chin. "You love it here."

I wipe the bubbles away. "I love it when you're here with me. It's lonely and boring when I'm here by myself."

"I'd love to have a few weeks just to myself," he says. "You should count yourself lucky."

"Then why don't you stay?" I say. "It's been, what, over two weeks since I left? That's plenty of time for you to sort things out and live here full-time."

He laughs as though I'm a small child repeating fairy tales. "That's really not that much time. And I can't just quit. We're going to need money to support the baby."

"I know." I feel frustrated, unable to express everything I'm thinking. "You could at least stay with me every night."

He puts his hands on either side of my face, a gesture he does when he's trying to keep me calm. "Everything I'm doing right now is for you and the baby. It won't be much longer. I promise."

And yet, more time passes. He comes every few nights, always having an excuse for why he can't be here. He never brings my charger. My phone has been dead for weeks. My only communication with the outside world, with the world I'd known before, are dull books that remind me of Emily, and I'm getting bored of that.

"I need to see a doctor," I say to him one morning, as he's getting ready to leave. "We have to make sure everything is okay with the baby."

"I told you, I'm trying to arrange for a physician to come here," he says. "You deserve the best care. You're more likely to pick up a bug in a waiting room this time of year."

"Why can't I just go into a normal clinic?" And then it dawns on me. "You still haven't told anyone about the baby. You're not trying to change your life back home at all."

"That isn't true—"

"Then why are you keeping me here alone? Like I'm some secret?" Especially now that Emily knows.

I hope the conversation will help him see things from my perspective, but it only pushes him away.

He starts coming to the house less and less frequently. He says he is busy with work, but how often can he use the same excuses? If I were his priority, he'd be here, wouldn't he?

Four days pass without a visit and I'm sick of it. I decide it's time to leave. There's no car here, but I'll walk into town and call an Uber, if that's what I must do. I can't be alone for another second.

I throw what few belongings I have into my suitcase and lumber downstairs. When I go to open the front door, it doesn't budge. It's locked, the doorknob barely even turning. Panic seizes every part of my body, but only temporarily. It must be a mistake. He probably locked the door without even thinking about it.

And yet, there's a part of me that wonders if the locked door is intentional. That idea terrifies me. This space might as well be a coffin, holding me in, making it difficult for me to breathe.

I rush to the sliding glass door on the other side of the house. It's locked, too, but it would be easy to escape. Escape. The use of the word makes the whole situation feel far more dramatic than it is. I start second-guessing myself. Sure, I'm mad that he hasn't been here in a few days, but if I throw a tantrum and break the sliding glass door, it'll make me look crazy. If I start acting irrational, he'll never pick me. And then what will I do? How will that benefit the baby?

Unsure of how to react, I sit in the living room, my suitcase beside me. I check the time. Already it's getting late. All I can do is wait.

# THIRTY-THREE

## EMILY

I wait in the foyer, watching as Byron gets in his car to leave. As he drives away, I wonder, could it have been his car I saw the night Rosie was left behind? Were they his taillights fading in the distance?

It takes a few hours to get Rosie settled. Once she's asleep in her bassinet, I pour a glass of wine and begin sifting through the boxes Byron left on my front porch. Bringing all this evidence is a show of good faith, but he could have easily left out anything leading back to him.

I can't believe I'm actually thinking this, that Byron could be involved. But until I have more answers, I can't trust anyone.

I begin by retracing all the information received in the early weeks of Erin's disappearance. At the time, it felt like an emotional tsunami but it quickly stalled after those initial weeks. Most cases are like that, it seems, or so I've come to believe after years of working in journalism. People uncover every detail, some relevant and some not, soon after a crime has been committed, then everything stops.

There are several pictures of Adam.

I open a manila folder labeled *Tips*. It takes a few moments for me to realize what I'm reviewing. It's all the phone tips from the police hotline that was set up during the first few weeks after Erin disappeared. How did Byron even get these? One of his reporter buddies must have done him a favor.

My eyes scan the document, countless names and phone numbers followed by miscellaneous details.

For the next several hours, I go over every call. Most of them are innocuous. Tips about people seeing someone who looks like Erin in states as far away as Massachusetts and Arizona. As unlikely as these leads are, I try to imagine Erin in those places. Living another life, maybe with Rosie by her side. But then how did her daughter get back here?

My phone rings. I look on the screen to see Marco is calling, surprising given how late it is. It isn't common for him to call me out of the blue.

"Any news?" I ask.

"None that you're going to be happy about," he says. "Why didn't you tell me that the baby left on your doorstep was related to Erin?"

My stomach drops and I feel the beginning of a migraine coming on. "You know why."

"The story about Erin's child is about to break. I want to give you a heads-up." He pauses. "As much as I want to hold it, I won't be able to do so much longer."

I understand. Marco has done everything within his power to help me in the wake of Erin's disappearance but sitting on a story like this could jeopardize his job. I can't ask him to do that.

"Is this conversation on record or off?"

"On record," he says. "Is there anything you can tell me?"

"Just that there are significant developments when it comes to Erin's case."

"And off record?" he asks.

"That there are too many questions and not enough answers," I say. "The baby is five months old, which means Erin was alive at least five months ago. But beyond that, I don't know anything. Where she's been the past year or how the baby got here."

"This David guy you asked me to look into," he says. "How does he play into everything?"

I sigh. "They've asked some of the men Erin was in contact with to submit paternity tests. Have you found anything out about him?"

"Nothing you can't find online." He pauses. "I read some campus rumors about him on an old student thread, but his criminal record is clean, at least."

He may not have the tumultuous past Adam has, but he still had reason to want Erin out of the way to protect himself if their affair restarted.

"It's good they're testing for paternity," Marco says. "Adam must be on their list."

"They already tested him," I say, defeated. "He's not a match."

"Wow. That's... unexpected."

Again, the former reporter in me stirs, imagining just how big a story this is going to be. Sure, it could shed more light on Erin's case, but it's also sensational enough to put me, and Rosie, under scrutiny. Maybe even in danger.

"Are you okay?" Marco asks. "Are you safe?"

"Yes."

"I'm worried about you."

"Worry about your story," I tell him, jokingly. "And that's all you're getting out of me."

I get off the phone and continue looking through the information in the boxes. I focus on the tips local to our area. They're more likely to be connected. Soon, one grabs my attention. It's a tip from someone in the area. A sighting of Erin within the first week after her disappearance.

It mentions a cabin.

I recall my conversation with Adam at the gazebo. He talked about Erin's fantasy life. How she envisioned a peaceful life at a cabin.

It's a small detail, but it could mean something. It's the first connection I've seen, and a weak one at that, but it could be worth exploring.

I look at the name of the caller; thankfully, it's not one of the dozens of anonymous tips that came in. This person's name and address is clearly listed. My heart stalls. Based on the information provided, I know where the cabin is located. Only a few miles away from my house. It's a place that Erin and I used to visit in the summers whenever our extended family came to town.

The weeks we had family visit during the summers were some of the only happy moments of my childhood. Those were the only times Mom would slow down her drinking and put effort into parenting. She'd dress us in coordinating outfits, braid my hair and put Erin's into pigtails. She wanted to showcase to her relatives that we were a happy family, even if that was far from reality.

I remember a lake in that area. Erin and I would take turns swinging from the rope swing tethered to a tree branch before leaping into the waters below. The first time she jumped, she was scared. I encouraged her to do it. Promised I'd be right there beside her when she let go.

I think of the countless tips received in the wake of Erin's disappearance. The story about Rosie being Erin's child will likely result in another wave, the vast majority of which will only cause confusion. That creates more pressure to figure out what's really happened before more irrelevant information starts muddying the waters.

I check the time. I'm lucky Rosie has let me work this long uninterrupted. I need to get some sleep. Tomorrow morning, I'm going to find out exactly where that tip came from.

# THIRTY-FOUR

The next morning, as I'm packing Rosie's bag, there's a knock on the front door.

Every time I hear that innocuous sound, I'm reminded of the night when Rosie came into my life. Now, she stirs in her bassinet, edging toward wakefulness. I scoop her in my arms and head downstairs.

Before opening the door, I peer out the narrow window to see who's on the porch. I can't think of who would be coming by this early, especially without calling. I'm surprised and elated to see Detective Carson.

"Is this a bad time?" he says, nodding at the baby. I see there's another officer with him. A woman I've never seen before.

"Rosie just woke up," I say.

"Rosie." He lets the name settle for a moment. "You decided on a name."

"Not official or anything. Just felt weird saying *baby* all the time." I'm suddenly charged by the idea this visit was prompted by a break in the case. "Did you get David's DNA test results back?"

Carson sighs and looks away. "He wasn't a match."

My heart sinks, as does my enthusiasm over the visit. What's the point of coming over if there aren't any new developments?

"You could have told me that over the phone," I say, defeated. I look behind him, making a point to nod at the other officer. "Do you have news about Erin?"

Carson looks behind him. "This is my partner, Detective Stevens. It would probably be best if we sit down."

I take a step back to let them both in. I hold Rosie close to my chest, suddenly alarmed. He didn't confirm whether he was here to discuss Erin, but the fact he wants to come inside suggests it's serious. My mind plays through scenarios. News that they've found a body, that there are no answers in terms of what might have happened to her, but she's gone nonetheless. It's as though I can feel the fresh threads of hope being ripped away from me.

By the time we enter the living room, my thoughts have sent me in a tizzy, my movements jerky. My throat feels as though it is closing in on itself as I wait for one of them to speak.

"When was your last communication with Adam?" Carson asks.

My body relaxes slightly. If they were here to break some kind of awful news about Erin, surely they would have led with that. "A couple days ago."

"When exactly?" Detective Stevens jumps in. This is the first time I've heard her speak.

I look between the detectives. "The day his DNA results came back. I felt he was on the verge of telling me something at the police station, so I hunted him down to find out what it was."

"Hunted?"

"Maybe that word is a little extreme," I say. "I went to his apartment to have a conversation. I already told you about this over the phone."

Carson nods. "What day and time was this? Exactly."

I tell them. "Adam said he'd been helping Erin this entire time, but it doesn't make sense. I don't understand why she would go to him and not me."

"So, you think Adam is lying?" Stevens asks.

"Of course he's lying," I say. "For a year, I've believed he's responsible for Erin's disappearance. I still think that. He's only changing his story now because Rosie is in the picture."

The detectives look at each other, then back at me. Or maybe they're looking at Rosie, watching as she tugs on the ends of my hair.

"Did anyone else witness your conversation?"

"Witness?" Such a strange way to phrase the question. "We sat at his gazebo in the middle of the day. There were people around nearby, but it was a private conversation."

"Did Adam invite you into his apartment?"

"No." I'm starting to get frustrated. "Well, he did, but I insisted we meet outside. Look, what is this about? How does this relate to Erin?"

"We're still looking into your sister's case," Carson assures me, "following up every lead, including the information you said you gathered from Adam. But that's not why we're here."

"Okay?" I say, growing more irritated.

Detective Stevens re-enters the conversation. "We're here because Adam was found dead, and foul play was involved."

The shock of her response makes me feel as though I've been drenched with icy water. I'm stunned. Out of all the scenarios going through my head, Adam's death wasn't one of them. I blink rapidly, hardly able to believe it. "When?"

"Coroner estimates he died two days ago," Stevens says. "The same day you went to visit him."

"Adam is dead." Rosie suddenly feels unbearably heavy. I

sit on the couch, leaning against the backrest as she squirms in my lap. "How?"

"Blunt force trauma," Carson says. "He was hit on the head with an extremely heavy object and bled out. We didn't find him until yesterday, when I went to ask him about what you told me during our phone call."

I shudder at the thought that someone I spoke with just days ago has been murdered. I recall the nervous energy I had as I sat beside him under the gazebo, grilling him about Erin. That icy sensation returns as I realize why they're here. "Do you suspect I have something to do with Adam's death?"

The detectives look at each other again before Stevens says, "You were with the victim on the day he died."

"That doesn't mean anything."

"The day before that you had a very heated exchange with him in front of half the police department," Carson says.

"Nothing happened," I say. "You interrupted us."

"For a year, you've maintained Adam murdered your sister because he was the last person seen with her," Stevens says, pointedly. "I don't think you can wave this off as nothing."

My cheeks flush. "We know he didn't kill Erin that night." I cut my eyes over to the baby. "Rosie proves that."

"You had a complicated history with him," Carson adds. "And you were with him on the day he died."

"I blamed him for what happened to Erin," I say, closing my eyes. "I wouldn't kill him."

"Is there anything else you can tell us about the day you saw him?"

I shake my head. Words and phrases sit on the tip of my tongue but refuse to coordinate. I'm hyper-focused on their tone and body language, on everything they've said leading up to this moment. Adam is dead, and they consider me a suspect. Piercing dread needles the back of my neck.

"We'll be in touch," Stevens says, walking toward the door.

The abrupt departure further startles me, as if they're intentionally dangling their threats in front of me. My ears begin to burn.

I stand quickly. "What about Erin?"

Carson stops before he exits the house and says, "We're still investigating, but things just got a lot more complicated."

Of course they did, I think. An active murder investigation certainly trumps a cold missing person's case.

And the police think I'm to blame.

# THIRTY-FIVE

## ERIN

Twenty Days Missing

When he returns later that night, I let him experience my full rage.

"I tried to leave earlier and the door was locked," I tell him. "From the outside."

He goes into the kitchen, starts unloading the groceries.

"Leave?" he says. "Why would you do that?"

"I think you're missing the point," I say. "Why would you lock me inside?"

Pulling a corkscrew from a drawer, he opens a bottle of wine. He pours a large glass and takes a sip before answering. "I'm not locking you in. I'm keeping people out."

"What people?" I say. "There's hardly anyone around—"

"You've not been following the news," he says. "There have been break-ins in this area. Several. I don't want to worry about something happening to you while I'm gone."

"Then maybe you shouldn't be gone so long."

He takes another sip of wine. Since when did he start drinking again? He promised me he'd stay sober.

"What if there was an emergency here? A fire?"

"If something like that were to happen, I imagine you'd break the sliding door," he says, nodding into the other room. "In a real emergency, I'm sure you could find your way out."

My jaw clenches as I consider I thought of that very thing earlier. Maybe I should have shattered the glass and started heading toward town. Maybe that would make him realize how desperate I am for things to change.

"We're supposed to be doing this together," I say to him. "I'm tired of being here night after night on my own."

"I only need a little more time," he says.

"How much more time could you possibly need?" I ask. "It's been weeks. People are starting to wonder where I am, surely."

He promised everyone believes what I told Adam, that I am taking time for myself. Even though Emily is upset, she must be worried about me now. She should be wanting to see me. Demanding it.

"I thought we wanted it this way," he says, his tone tender. "You and me against the world."

It had been romantic at first, ideal. But now I want out of this fantasy. I want back to my old life where, even if things are difficult, I'll be able to make a way for myself. In some of my darkest moments, I've even thought about being a single mother. I've been scared of the idea because of my experiences as a child, but I wouldn't be like Mom, no matter what Emily says. Sooner or later, she'll have to forgive me. She can't avoid me forever, especially when there is a child involved. I realize that now.

I could do this on my own, without him, if that's what it takes.

"I'm ready to go home," I tell him. "I want you to take me to my apartment. I'm not going to play along with this anymore."

I am crying fiercely, losing control of my own emotions. Pregnancy has made me feel everything so closely.

"I've been drinking," he says, nodding at the empty glass of wine. "I don't want to drive right now."

"No, you don't want to be with me."

"That isn't true!" he shouted. "I'm willing to give up everything for you and the baby. I just need a little more time."

I start to feel guilty. I have no idea how difficult it must be for him to break ties with the life he's built. Maybe I am asking too much. All this time alone has done more than just relax me; it has deteriorated my brain. Made me paranoid.

He puts his hand over mine. "Let's call it a night. We both need rest. In the morning, we'll drive into town together. We can make a doctor's appointment. I can take you to your apartment. Whatever you want, just to show you I'm telling the truth."

It is always hard for me to stay angry with him. We go upstairs, falling asleep in the master bedroom. I feel so whole with his arms wrapped around me. At peace.

* * *

The next morning, I feel his absence right away. I startle up in bed, afraid he lied to me once again, that he's gone into town and left me behind. I am relieved when I see him walking out of the bathroom, fixing his tie.

"You're still here," I say, rising to greet him.

That's when I notice the tug on my arm. Something holding me in place. I look at my right side, and I have to blink several times to make sense of what I'm seeing, make sure it's not some mirage.

There's a handcuff around my wrist, tethering me to the bedpost. I yank on the chain, each movement seeming to clasp the cuff even tighter around me.

"What is this?" I say, forcing a nervous laugh. "Some kind of prank?"

He sits on the foot of the bed, staring at me with a blank expression.

"Erin, we need to talk," he says. "Things are about to change."

# THIRTY-SIX

## EMILY

I'm jumpy as I pace around the house, trying to soothe Rosie into a nap. She must sense my frustration, and that's why she's fighting me.

I can't believe that Adam is dead.

I lied earlier when I told the police I'd never wanted to kill him. I've thought about it. Every time I caught him walking out of his apartment, going about his life like everything was fine. Each time I followed his car out to the woods, wondering if he was memorializing what had happened there with my sister.

I wanted to hurt him because I believed he'd killed Erin, but now nothing is making sense.

The only thing I know for a fact is that I had nothing to do with Adam's death, not that the police are going to take my word for it. Who would have wanted to kill him? And why would his death come so soon after Rosie appeared?

It makes me wonder if he was telling the truth after all. If Erin believed she was in danger, and that looping me in would somehow cause me harm, maybe there's a reason she hasn't reached out in the past year. Maybe Adam got too close, and that's why someone killed him.

I told anyone that would listen I thought Erin's case was a classic situation of domestic abuse. Even earlier this week, when I sat down with Marco, I talked about how I believed Adam was to blame. The article that came out earlier this week all but accused him. If someone feared people were getting closer to the truth, Adam would be a natural target.

Which only means I'm in the crosshairs too.

Paranoia looms. Adam's sudden death is a reminder how fragile life is. We had a simple conversation outside his apartment, and some hours later he was bludgeoned to death. The house feels too large, the isolation from the city overwhelming. I scoop up Rosie's things into the diaper bag and head to my car. It doesn't matter where I'm going; I'll feel safer if I'm not alone.

My phone rings. Byron is calling.

When I answer, he exhales, and I can't decide whether he sounds relieved or not. "Adam is dead."

"I know," I say. "I got a visit from Carson and another detective just now." I pause. "How do you know about it?"

"I work at a newspaper, remember? Small-town murders certainly capture our attention." He sighs. "I told you it was dangerous reaching out to him on your own."

"I'm fine, aren't I?"

My own arrogance annoys me. As brave as I might try to act with Byron, I am afraid for my safety. And Rosie's. It's the reason I'm scrambling to get out of the house.

"Adam's death makes everything more dangerous," he says. "You and Rosie shouldn't be on your own."

"Well, I don't really have anyone else I can trust," I say, recalling how we left things the other night.

"What did the police say to you?"

I provide the limited information the police shared, ending with the fact they think I could be involved.

"That's ridiculous," he says. "I was with you later that night. We had dinner. It wouldn't be hard to give them an alibi."

"I know."

"I'm more worried about what this could mean for you and Rosie," he says. "If Adam was murdered, it has to be tied to Erin. Either whoever she was running from became worried he knew too much, or they followed you."

I had the same thought earlier. A shiver goes up my spine. "I know."

Byron is quiet for several minutes. I wonder what he's thinking, if that analytical mind of his is toying with different possibilities. Suspects. Or maybe he's trying to cover his own tracks.

"I don't think it's safe for you to be on your own. Not after what happened to Adam. Why don't the two of you come stay at my place?"

"There's not enough room."

"We'll make room. If someone is stalking you, they're probably watching the house. They may not yet know about my apartment."

"I'll tell you when I come up with a plan," I say, ending the call.

I still don't know if I can fully trust Byron. Besides, there are bigger things for me to worry about. The police may consider me a suspect in Adam's murder, but nothing, not even Adam's death, will stop me from looking into the lead I uncovered last night.

Suddenly, I know exactly where I need to go. The cabin.

# THIRTY-SEVEN

The sun beams brighter as I drive away from the city, toward the forest. Light filters through the trees overhead, casting shadows on the road.

I recall making this journey several times in the past year, always following Adam. Sometimes he'd seem to drive around aimlessly, and I wondered if he was thinking about his last night with Erin, what he did to her.

Now, he's dead. And it appears that the person I thought was responsible for taking my sister didn't do it. He claimed he was only trying to help. Nothing makes sense. I only hope that today's visit will give me some answers.

Rosie lets out a cry in the back seat. For a moment, I forgot she was with me. I debated whether I should bring her at all. If I think this could be connected to Erin's disappearance, I don't want to put her in danger. And yet, there's no one I can ask to watch her. Viv and Matt have done more than enough for me in recent days, and leaving her alone with Byron feels too risky.

He still never told me if he was willing to submit to a DNA test.

My car's GPS dings, instructing me to turn right. It's a

narrow, one-lane driveway, a gravel runway in the middle of bright-green grass. I drive along this path for several minutes and begin to fear I've taken a wrong turn. Sometimes these rural addresses don't mesh with modern technology, and it's easy to get lost.

I'm relieved when the gravel road turns into pavement. A few minutes later, I pull into a clearing. It looks like a cul-de-sac, although there are only three houses lining the semicircle. The lake sits on the other side of the houses.

I park in the middle of the cul-de-sac and step out of my car. I'm immediately taken aback by how fresh the air feels. Clean and crisp, far different from what I'm used to in the middle of town. The sun warms my shoulders, and it's like I'm being transported through time, back to one of the summers when Erin and I were children.

Taking Rosie from her car seat, I strap her to my body using one of the contraptions I bought during my shopping spree. It takes a few minutes to make sure I'm using it correctly, but once I stand upright, I can feel Rosie heavy and secure against my chest.

Overhead, a bird caws, reminding me of what I'm here to do. I survey the three houses nearby. They have a similar style, likely made by the same construction company, but there are subtle differences. Metal roofs versus tile, porch columns or a fence. The house closest to me, my destination, has a large American flag hanging from the front door, patriotic colors dancing in the breeze.

Cautiously, I approach the steps. An older man opens the door. He wears a checkered button-up shirt beneath a burgundy cardigan, despite the warm weather outside. When he sees me, his eyes squint, as though trying to place me in his mind.

"Do I know you?" he says, his voice scratchy.

"No, sir."

Before I can say anything else, he adds, "No salespeople." He begins to shut the door.

"I'm not trying to sell anything," I say quickly. Rosie begins kicking her legs, causing me to shift my weight. "I don't want to bother you at all. I only want to ask a few questions."

"Questions," he says, unamused. His eyes linger on Rosie and his demeanor softens.

"Yes. It's been a while, but did you call a police tip line with information about a missing person?"

"Missing person? What are you on about?" He steps onto the porch. "Are you police?"

"It's fine, Grandpa." A younger man exits the house. He must be younger than me, in his twenties. "I was the one who called."

"Why would you do that?" he says.

"See something, say something." He looks back at me, returning to his grandfather's question from earlier. "Are you the police?"

"No. The woman you called about. The one who went missing," I say, squeezing Rosie's little hand to calm my own anxieties. "I'm her sister."

The younger man's face stills, unsure of how to react. The older gentleman continues watching me suspiciously.

"Anyway," I say, trying to get the words out before I'm cut off again, "I've been going through some old tips, and came across your information. You called it in not long after she went missing. Almost a year ago. You might not even remember."

"I remember it well," the young man says. "I'm studying criminal justice in school." He holds out his hand to shake mine. "Name's Justin, by the way."

The old man throws his hands in the air, bored of our conversation, and walks back into the house. Justin comes outside, joining me on the porch.

"Is there anything else you can tell me about what you saw?"

"I wasn't exactly the person who saw it," he says.

"What?"

"I mean, I did see a girl. I just didn't get that good of a look at her," he says, pausing long enough to give Rosie a charmed smile. "My buddy who was staying with me for the week saw her better and said she looked like the missing girl from the news."

"Tell me exactly what happened," I say, reaching inside my purse and retrieving my old journalist's notepad.

Justin inhales and looks at the sky, as though trying to remember.

"You know that music festival a couple hours from here? It was the week before that, which is why I'm able to remember precisely. A bunch of my friends from college stayed overnight here. We figured it was a good stopping point on the way." He nods back toward the house. "Grandpa isn't always this grumpy."

I nod, urging him to continue.

"We stayed a couple nights. On our second day, we decided to rent some kayaks and head out on the lake." He turns to look at the water in front of us. "We were out there for a couple hours, just playing around. We even floated by our cabin, and that's when we saw her.

"My friend pointed her out to me. Said she was really pretty. By the time I looked, she was turned around. All I saw was her dress. Black with some kind of white pattern on it."

"That's it," I say. "You were kayaking on the lake and saw a girl?"

"I know, it's not important. I didn't even think of it until a couple days later, when we were driving back through town. We stayed the night here again and caught the local news. They were going on and on about a missing woman. My friend recognized her as the girl from the lake immediately."

"You made the call," I say. "If your friend saw Erin, why didn't he call it in?"

"My buddies can get kind of weird around cops. Never mind the fact I want to be one someday." He shakes his head. "Anyway, I told him he should ring the tip line. He didn't want to, so I did it myself."

I nod, grateful he decided to call it in, even if it appears not much will come from it. I pull out my phone, scrolling through pictures.

"I know you said you didn't get a good look of her face," I say, holding up a recent picture of Erin, "but do you recognize her?"

He shakes his head. "Sorry. My buddy said it was her, that's all."

I scroll through the other pictures on my phone, until I find one of Erin wearing a dress similar to the one he described. My heart seizes when I realize the picture was taken on the night she went missing, a selfie we snapped right before entering the restaurant.

"What about this dress?"

He stares at the photo. "I think that's it. I mean, it was a year ago. But I swear, that's the person we saw."

"And she was by the lake?"

He nods. "Just standing right there." He points to a patch of grass between the other two houses.

I scan my surroundings, considering the remote road that led me here.

"Why would she be here?" I ask, under my breath. "Do you know anything about your grandfather's neighbors?"

"He doesn't really have them," he says, nodding to either side of him. "I mean, the other two houses are rentals only. That's why Grandpa's so mean to strangers. He gets a new round of renters every few months or so. Weekly in the summer."

"Rentals?"

"Yeah. You know, they're listed on one of those home sites. Vacation Homes Online, something like that."

"If she was staying there with someone, you wouldn't know anything about it?"

He shrugs. "Like I said, my grandpa is the only person here full-time. Most of the year, those places are empty."

There are dozens of possibilities running through my mind. Did Erin get abducted by someone who was staying at one of the rental houses? Or did she rent it herself and that's where her money went? Could Adam have been lying this whole time? Could he have brought her here and then done something to her? But if that's true, who killed him?

"I'm really sorry about your sister," Justin says. "I wish I could do more to help."

"You've done a lot actually," I say, trying to make him feel better. "You did the right thing in calling it in."

That compliment seems to cheer him up. He smiles before going back inside.

I walk down the wooden steps, looking at the other two houses. Both appear vacant right now. No cars are in the driveway, and I can't see an attached garage. The house in the center still has a holiday wreath on the front door. No one must have rented the place in a long time. Maybe the police would be able to investigate if this house was rented the week Erin went missing.

Before returning to my car, I walk closer to the lake. I take off my shoes, enjoying the sensation of wet grass and soil beneath my feet. The trickling water is calm and peaceful. The clouds drift through the sky. I picture Erin being here, if it was her at all. What would she have been thinking in that precise moment when Justin and his friend saw her?

Was she scared, trying to escape? Or was she at peace, happy?

And what is she experiencing now? Relief that she no longer has a baby to care for. Grief over the fact her child was taken from her. Is she even alive at all?

The breeze brushes past me, pushing the hair away from my face. Rosie stirs against my chest, burrowing her head closer to me for warmth. I get the sense that Erin is here with us, which doesn't bring me much peace. I've had this feeling a few different times over the past year but always wished it away. I didn't need any kind of sign suggesting my sister was no longer alive.

And yet now, as I look across the water, contemplating whether today's conversation has brought me any closer to her, I feel her with me. I realize a part of her will always be with me, whether I find out what happened to her or not. The thought brings tears to my eyes.

# THIRTY-EIGHT

## ERIN

Seven Months Missing

I thought he loved me, but with each passing, monotonous day, I become more and more aware that this isn't love.

Lately, he's not even trying to hide his annoyance. He no longer kisses me, caresses me, calms me with sweet nothings in my ear. Ever since telling me the plan, he's treated me as nothing more than an incubator. He cares about the baby and nothing else.

These are the thoughts that cloud my mind over the next several months, as I watch my stomach grow from the size of a small pear to a round basketball.

*He doesn't love you.*

*He never loved you.*

*It's all about the baby. The plan.*

And yet, there's that voice inside of me that doesn't want it to be true. I want to believe that he loves me, that the fantasy life we set out to build together will still come to fruition.

And then I look at the handcuffs on my wrist.

He checks on me less frequently. He provides me with

anything I might need during his absence. Water, food, blankets. A bedpan. And yet, none of that can substitute for my lack of human connection. With each passing day, I miss my old life more. I miss Emily. I miss him—the man I thought I knew.

The baby is the only person I speak to from one day to the next. I've gotten in the habit of calling him or her Little Bit; it's a name I remember Emily calling me when I was a toddler.

I tell Little Bit stories about my childhood, about Aunt Emily, about him. I leave out the part where he has me chained to a headboard, hoping the child can't already sense my endless levels of stress and despair.

I recite positive affirmations, anything that can trick my baby into thinking it's entering a healthy environment instead of the toxic situation I'm facing.

*You are so loved, Little Bit.*

*We're going to have a beautiful life together.*

*It's you and me against the world, Little Bit.*

And then, it happens. A sharp pain in my stomach, one that feels different from the normal stretches and gas bubbles I'm used to feeling. This sensation is heavier, like something inside me is dropping. Wetness spreads on the sheets around me.

I spend the next few hours in a panic, one contraction leading into another. There's no clock here. I have no way of timing when the next one might arrive, and the pain seems to endure for hours.

In between my worry and fear and pain, I'm angry at him for leaving me. There's no way I can do this on my own, one hand chained to the bedpost.

"We're going to get through this, Little Bit," I say aloud, still trying to comfort my child in between uneven breaths.

The contractions are only minutes apart when I hear a sound. A door closing. He's here. In that second, all my anger evaporates; I'm just so happy to not be alone.

He walks into the room, his face turning pale when he sees me on the bed. "How long has this been happening?"

"Hours," I say. "You have to take me to a hospital."

"I can't."

Every muscle in my body tightens, my full fury and rage settling in. For what seems to be the first time, I'm seeing him for who he is. A coward. Someone who only cares about himself. He's more worried about what could happen to him than he is about the baby, about me.

Anger pushes me to lash out, hurt him so that he can understand the heartache he's put me through, but I don't have the luxury of giving into my emotions. Another earthquake of pain rattles through me. Tears stream down my cheeks as I try my best to breathe through the agony.

"I've been studying what to do," he says, kneeling in front of me on the bed. He unlocks the handcuff. Maybe he's ashamed. "I didn't think it would happen this fast."

He's right. As impossible as it is to keep track of time, it doesn't seem like seven months have passed. Have I really been a prisoner that long? I wonder what my friends and family and colleagues back home think. Do they think I'm dead? Do they care?

Another contraction sends me shuddering, and even though I'm completely unaware of what to do, an instinctual part of me understands the time is near. The baby is coming.

She comes quickly. It's not as drawn out as it seems to be in the movies, as it was portrayed during those soap operas I used to watch as a kid, but it's certainly painful. I feel like my body is ripping from the inside out, my breath inadequate to keep me going.

He puts his hands on my legs, trying to comfort me, trying to help. I both crave and resent his touch.

It comes quickly, the fragile cry ringing out into the room, reaching inside me and filling that part of me that has been broken for so long.

He holds the baby in his arms, smiling. "It's a girl."

I smile. My body aches for her, like I never knew it was possible to live without her, even though we've only just met. I raise my arms.

"Can I—"

"Let me clean her up," he says, cutting me off. He stands quickly, carrying the baby into the bathroom. I didn't even get the chance to hold her.

Still out of breath, my body trembling in the aftershocks of labor, I stare at his phone. He's left it at the foot of the bed, and in the chaos of the moment, he doesn't realize it.

He doesn't realize I'm still unchained either.

I take the phone and unlock the screen. There's only one bar of service. I begin dialing furiously. It doesn't occur to me to call 911. I'm not worried about myself. I'm worried about letting my loved ones know I'm okay.

Emily is the first person who comes to mind. Ah, how I've missed her voice! I remember what he told me about her reaction to my letter. Over the past few months, I've wondered if it's true, if he even gave her my note, but part of me fears that it is. I'm afraid Emily really did say those things about me and won't care about me or Little Bit.

I recall the only other number I know by heart: Mom's. It's funny how the numbers you memorize in childhood stay with you the rest of your life.

I'm elated when I hear the ringing, and again when I hear her voice.

"Mom! Help!" I shout into the receiver, thrilled for the chance to finally tell someone where I am, that I'm okay, that I have a daughter.

Something heavy and sharp strikes the top of my head, and the world turns black.

Cell phone service doesn't resume until I'm close to town. My phone begins buzzing, and Viv's name appears on the screen.

"Where the hell are you?" she says, sounding agitated.

"Running errands," I say.

"The story about Rosie broke just after lunch," she says, "Local news stations are eating it up. If I had to guess, I'd say they're at your house."

"Shit. Does the offer to stay at your place still stand?"

"Always," she says.

"I'm heading home first," I say, speeding in the direction of my house. I'll need to pick up some things.

Marco sends me a message a few minutes later, apologizing for the media storm his recent article caused. He's been put in an awkward position, forced to choose between doing his job and being a friend.

I don't fault him for anything that's happened. I leaned on him when most people were refusing to discuss Erin's case, when there were no leads in sight. It's not fair to blame him now that the case has more attention than we could have ever predicted.

Still, when I see the sheer amount of people parked outside my house, it's overwhelming. I only wanted to stop by to grab a few things, anything Rosie might need and an extra change of clothes for me. But there are news vans and civilian cars parked outside, making it difficult for me to enter my own driveway.

I pull the car into the garage, relief washing over me as I lower the bulky door, blocking out the chaos. I hurry through the house, grabbing anything we might need over the next few days. As I'm exiting the dining room, I spot the boxes Byron delivered yesterday, the ones containing all his research about Erin, including the tip at the cabin I just followed up on. I add those to the trunk of my car too before pulling out onto the street.

I understand the media's obsession with Rosie's existence. Like me, most of the world believed Erin was the victim of foul play, likely dead. To know she was alive and had a child is unbelievable. Or it would be, if there wasn't a bouncing baby girl in the back seat, lifting her tiny feet into the air.

Viv and Matt are wealthy enough that their large house is protected by high walls and a wrought-iron gate. No media will be able to get past it, giving us our best chance of privacy.

When I arrive, I enter the gate code, Viv and Matt's wedding date. I'm overwhelmed by the sense of safety that falls over me watching the bars close behind us. This might be the only place where we can hide from the press and those that wish us harm.

I drive along the paved road snaking uphill until we reach the house, a massive brick building with circular windows. Viv's car is in the driveway. She must be preparing for our arrival.

Byron and I have spent countless evenings here. It must be the least childproof place I've ever been. Expensive art and sculptures in every room. Several staircases. It's a reflection of their cosmopolitan lifestyle. Good thing Rosie is still too small to wander around. As long as she's in someone's arms, she'll be safe.

Viv comes out to greet us. "Happy you made it," she says. "I've fixed up the guest room."

"That's great, Viv," I say. "You're a lifesaver."

I hand her Rosie's carrier so I can take out the rest of the bags. Once inside, we settle Rosie inside the foldable pack and play I brought, and she quickly falls asleep.

"Can I get you anything?" Viv asks, standing in the doorway of the bedroom.

"Just going over some things," I tell her, pulling the box of Erin's belongings onto my bed.

"You know, I'm really proud of how you've handled everything in the past week," she says.

"What do you mean?"

"I always admired how you were there for Erin," she says. "But the way you've stepped up for Rosie... She's lucky to have you."

"It's not like I had much of a choice."

"But you did. You could have chosen not to get involved," she says. "Instead, you've doubled down on doing what's right."

I smile. "I'm lucky to have you and Matt. I'd be completely overwhelmed back at the house myself."

"I was thinking of heading downstairs to make dinner," she says. "Want to join me?"

"I'm going to stay up here until she finishes napping," I say.

She walks away and I begin looking through the boxes. I felt so close to Erin when I was standing on the banks of the lake, almost as though I could reach out and touch her. I keep believing that if I keep going, I might find something useful.

It's amazing that I've never seen some of these photos before. I imagine most of them were tacked onto her wall, a colorful collage of important moments and people. One picture captures my attention. It's Erin sitting in the grass, holding a small flower in her hands, but that's not what interests me.

It's the background behind her. A grassy embankment with rolling water in the back. I realize I've seen this area before. Earlier today, actually. This was taken in the same area as the cabin I visited.

I take out my phone, pulling up the picture I took of the lake. It's the exact same location, but this photo must have been taken months before she went missing, the same place where Justin's friend saw her and called in the tip.

Erin had been there before.

Maybe, I think, she's still there.

# FORTY

## ERIN

Twelve Months Missing

After the phone call, he moved me to the attic. That was my punishment. Now I have even less to entertain me, less to focus on. There's a window, but it's so far across the room I can't look out of it. I've never felt more removed from the rest of the world. Alone.

Except when I'm with her. Little Bit gives my life meaning. The way she nuzzles against my chest. Her eyes, so full of expression and curiosity and knowing, lock onto mine. Her tiny mouth latches around my breast when it's time for her to feed.

These precious moments are the only things that keep me going, that even make my isolation from the rest of the world seem worth it.

I dread his presence now more than ever. Whenever he comes, it's only so he can take the baby with him, and when he does that, it feels like my soul is being ripped away from me. I've tried crying, pleading, begging for her to stay, but he just reminds me of the plan.

Little Bit will never be mine to keep. I don't have the resources to support her, not like he does.

And yet, I want her so badly. There's a part of me that feels I'd be capable of overcoming anything this world could throw at me, if it means I could be with her.

It's hard to have choices and make grand plans when you're chained to a bed, a flimsy room divider blocking me from even seeing the farthest reaches of this attic. All I can do is value the present, be grateful for the moments I have with her, before he comes to take her again.

There's another part of the plan he's yet to tell me. He's too afraid, too weak, to admit what will happen once Little Bit no longer needs my breast milk. He won't leave me chained to this bed forever. He can't. Sooner or later, he's going to get rid of me. Little Bit will never know I'm her mother because I won't be around to raise her.

I never thought he was capable of doing this to me, to us, to her.

The back-and-forth is wearing hard on him. I see his exhaustion every time he comes to visit. The way he staggers into the room. The deep bags beneath his eyes. Caring for a newborn is difficult, and I imagine even more so when you're juggling the heavy weight of your other crimes.

He can't get rid of me yet. Little Bit needs my breast milk to survive. I wonder, sometimes, if he isn't stalling because he doesn't want to harm me. There must have been a part of him that loved me once. Maybe it's still buried deep in there. Or maybe I'm thinking like one of those soap opera fantasies I used to watch, and that spark fizzled out long, long ago.

He stomps up the stairs to the attic, each thud of his footsteps making me wild with anticipation. He's had Little Bit for over a day, the longest she's ever been gone from me. I can't wait to hold her again, feel her pudgy body melt into mine.

He hands her over, unlocking the chain around my wrist in silence. He always does this when I'm feeding her; a small shred of humanity, I suppose. Normally, he sits beside me on the bed, so there's no risk of me escaping, but tonight he appears even more frazzled than normal, more tired. He lies back on the bed, stretching his exhausted limbs, and falls asleep.

I don't even realize it myself, at first. Like him, I guess I'm becoming conditioned to my circumstances, falling into routine.

My left wrist is no longer handcuffed. He forgot. I move forward, Little Bit in my arms, trying my best to move quietly, unsure of what might happen next. My legs feel like jelly as I scamper across the room, pushing my bare feet into sneakers, my adrenaline driving me forward.

I climb carefully down the narrow attic ladder, holding the baby close to my chest. When I reach the main level, I spot the baby's carrier, the one I imagine he uses whenever he drives her in the car. I slip her inside, making sure she's secure and comfortable. Part of me wonders if I'm dreaming, hallucinating. Surely, after all the months I've been trapped here, it can't be that easy to escape.

Maybe he knows exactly what he's doing, and he only left me unchained as a test. When I reach the front door, it will be locked, and when he does return, whether it's tomorrow or days later, I'll receive a punishment even worse than last time.

But when I turn the front door handle, it swings open with ease, the cool night air rushing inside the cabin, filling my lungs with possibility and hope.

I can't believe I'm standing here, reunited with the world once again. And his car is right there. I rush back inside, searching for a set of keys, but I worry I'm making too much noise, wasting too much time. I can't risk waking him up and losing this opportunity.

I'm unchained. The door is unlocked. And my daughter is

safe in my arms. Maybe, this is the universe, giving me an opportunity after all this time.

I hold Little Bit tighter, staring into her deep blue eyes, a multitude of questions between us, and realize this could be my only chance.

If I'm going to escape, I have to go now.

# FORTY-ONE
## EMILY

Viv appears off-guard when I ask her to watch Rosie. She's already opened up her home to us, and now I'm enlisting her for babysitting services. Still, she agrees to do it without question.

"What do the police want to talk to you about?" she asks.

This is the excuse I gave her for why I needed to leave. I don't want to worry her about where I'm actually going, and I don't want to jinx the fact I might finally have a lead.

"I don't know," I tell her. "Maybe it has something to do with the article coming out."

"Or maybe they've found new evidence," she says, hopeful.

I bend down, kissing Rosie on the forehead. I wish, for a moment, that was the case. That the police had really reached out to me with new information instead of me tracking it down on my own.

"I'll call you when I'm on my way back," I say, asking Viv again if there's anything she needs. My eyes linger on Rosie a moment longer. I'm getting closer to finding out what happened to Erin, a monumental occurrence for the both of us.

*I'm going to find your mommy, sweet girl*, I think silently, before walking away.

The lake is farther from Viv and Matt's house than from downtown. For most of the drive, I'm lost in thought about the various possibilities surrounding Erin's disappearance. It doesn't appear any cars are following me, but there's still a level of fear in knowing I'm heading out here again by myself.

I consider Justin, the person who called in the tip. He seemed helpful earlier, but that could have been deceiving. Perpetrators like to insert themselves into investigations. Maybe he wasn't the person who called it in at all. Maybe the story he told me is flipped. His buddy called it in, and now he has to cover his tracks. I hadn't considered that possibility. The people pretending to help me could be just as threatening as anyone else.

I wish I knew when that picture was taken. More importantly, I wish I knew who took the picture, who joined her at the cabin. Erin never mentioned visiting the lake as an adult. We went there as kids. If she'd gone back, you'd think she would have told me. *Hey, remember that place we used to go during the summer? I went back there.* She didn't say anything.

Of course, as I've learned in the past week, this is low on the list of things she didn't tell me. Clearly, Erin had a ton of other secrets. The man she was dating. Her plans to leave town. The fact she was pregnant. I still can't believe Erin would hide all this from me without a good reason.

The gravel blends into the paved road. With the windows rolled down, I can hear the water as I approach. Soon, I reach the clearing with the three houses. I park in front of the one in the middle.

I pull out the picture I found and hold it up. The locations match almost exactly. Could this be it, or just another dead end? Am I any closer to finding Erin?

I raise my head, staring at the house. I imagine Erin standing to the left of it, closer to the lake, and someone snapping the photograph that's now in my hands. Who was here with her?

Without thinking, I march forward.

I climb the front porch. There's nothing personal about it. No friendly doormat, no decorative wreath. I'm surprised this place is a rental at all. It certainly doesn't look inviting. I work my way around the wraparound porch.

The back of the house has a large sliding glass door. I hold my hands up against the glass, trying to block out the glare so I can peek in. The inside of the house is as stereotypical as the outside. I see a rug on the floor, a stone fireplace and a leather sofa with a blanket draped over it. All the lights are off. No signs of life.

I feel my adrenaline and panic leaving me, a frightening feeling, like I'm close to jumping off the edge of a cliff only to be pulled back at the last minute. I look around, appreciating the cool breeze that sweeps the hair across my face. There can't be any more coincidences. No more dead ends. I must find out what happened, no matter the cost.

In the corner of the porch is a football-sized rock. Without thinking, I bend down to grab it, throwing it through the glass.

I brace for the sound of an alarm. When nothing starts blaring, I reach my hand through the hole and unlock the door. I slide it open, careful not to step on any fragments of glass as I walk inside.

It's cold inside the house. I can't help feeling like there's a lack of life. I flick on the lights, but even that doesn't add a layer of warmth. I walk through the living room, which is empty and barren, and make my way into the kitchen. It's just as impersonal in there. Very few items on the countertops, and a few high-top stools around a small table.

For a moment, I'm aware of how strange it is that I've entered on my own without permission. Broken in. That moment of rationality soon goes away, as I think about the reason I'm here. Erin.

I dart down the hallway to my left. The first door leads to a bathroom. The door beside it is a small storage closet. The last door leads to a bedroom with a large walk-in closet. There's another rustic rug covering the floors.

I walk over to the nightstand, and that's when I see it. A framed picture of my best friend and her husband. I hold it up, blinking away tears as I look at it.

This cabin belongs to Matt.

# FORTY-TWO

It feels like the room is spinning around me, the water rising from the lake to wash me away.

Viv and Matt own this house, the same house where one of the last known sightings of Erin took place. Byron and I have visited at their home numerous times over the years. They've never mentioned having a vacation home, although they're certainly wealthy enough to afford it. I wonder if Byron knows our friends have a lakeside home a few miles away from our house.

What does that mean, exactly? It can't be a coincidence. Erin was here before she went missing, sitting on the grass beside the water and I didn't know this place even existed. And she was spotted again months later, after she'd gone missing.

Does this mean Erin and Matt were having an affair? It would explain why she felt overwhelmed by her situation, why she needed to escape. She must have thought I'd never forgive her for sleeping with Matt. Her boss. My best friend's husband.

The revelation is unbelievable. We've all spent time together countless times away from the office. Matt always treated Erin like a little sister, like Byron and Viv and everyone else. In the wake of her disappearance, Matt was there to comfort me. Is it really possible he's known where she was this entire time?

The disloyalty would have started before that, whenever their affair began. I've never known him to be unfaithful before. What was he thinking, sleeping with a subordinate at the office? My sister? Does he realize how many boundaries this betrayal has broken?

My heart aches for Vivienne. When she finds out that Matt was having an affair and is involved in Erin's disappearance, she's going to be devastated. She was close to Erin, too, but the bond between us is unbreakable. Viv became my second sister when I left for college. I've watched her go through life. Fall in love. Grow her business into the empire it is today. And she's one of the people who was there for me the most after Erin went missing.

These thoughts thunder through my brain in a matter of seconds, but I quickly shoo them away. I can't think about any of that now. All that matters is finding Erin. If this is where she's been kept this entire time, maybe she's still here.

I race through the cabin, opening every bedroom and closet door. It isn't very big, a fraction of the size of their home back in the city. Every room I enter is empty, clean and unused. It looks as though no one has stayed here in months, making my hopes of finding Erin plummet. I lower my head and close my eyes, hoping this trek out here isn't a lost cause. There's been a trail of clues leading me here: the tip line, the photograph. This place belongs to Viv and Matt. All those connections must mean something. My heart can't handle another dead end.

I enter the walk-in closet connected to the master bedroom, seeing nothing but rows of clothing and folded up blankets, and I fear I'm running out of places to search. I look up in frustration, and that's when I see it. A small rectangle with a string dangling down.

There's an attic.

I pull on the cord and the rectangle creaks open. A retractable ladder slides down. I extend the wooden steps as far as they will go, testing them for durability.

My back and thighs ache as I climb the narrow ladder. I remain crouched down, afraid I'll hit my head on something if I stand up fully. The wood feels unsteady as I rise higher and higher toward the ceiling.

It's dark inside the attic. I reach for my phone, using the torch to look overhead. Another string dangles right above me. I pull on it, and light fills the space.

Dust motes float through the air like snow. There's nothing more than storage boxes. At the center of the wall is a small circular window. It faces the lake, which is impossible to see from the front of the house.

Beneath it is a room divider, blocking what's on the other side from view. I turn the corner.

There's a narrow bed. A small nightstand with a lamp. A metal bedpan overturned on the floor. I step closer, my eyes scanning the area for more details. It doesn't make sense these items would be stored here in the attic, arranged in this precise way.

The linens are rumpled, as though someone got out of bed and never returned. Something strange catches my attention. I reach out, my entire body shuddering when my fingers graze the cool, dull metal.

Handcuffs. There's a set connected to a longer metal chain attached to the bed's headboard. My heart starts beating faster as the reality of what took place here enters my mind.

Erin was here. After all these months of searching, I've finally found where she was kept, but now she's gone.

I'm too late.

# FORTY-THREE

## ERIN

Twelve Months Missing

When I step outside, it's like being swallowed up by another universe.

How long has it been since I left the attic? The house? Several months, at least. I'm overcome by the sensations around me. The cool night breeze, the burbling water in the distance. Even the moon seems impossibly bright, makes me wonder if I'm imagining this entire moment.

Little Bit wriggles in her carrier, her movement bringing me back to the present.

Whatever I plan on doing, I must act fast. Before he wakes up, before he realizes I'm gone.

I walk forward, the light from the moon shining on the path in front of me. Beyond that, it's impossibly dark, hard for me to make out anything around me. Still, I know this area. It's where Emily and I used to vacation when we were younger. Her house is only a few miles from here, I know. If I keep along the road, maybe I can make it there.

For every step forward, there's a fear holding me back.

I imagine how angry he'll be when he realizes I'm gone. On the night Little Bit was born, he was so upset with me for using the phone, he hurt me, locked me in the attic for months. When he finds out I've left the house with the baby, there's no predicting what he'll do. Whatever has been preventing him from killing me will no longer exist. I could very well be marching toward my execution.

And yet, that's only if he does wake up, if he does find me. I tell myself to keep moving, each passing moment bringing me hope.

It's frightening out here all alone, different from the fear I'm used to experiencing at the cabin. There, it's all the what-ifs and maybes that terrify me. In the wilderness, I consider all the other potential threats. Rugged terrain and hungry animals and slithering reptiles. Lugging the baby beside me, I try not to think about it, continue putting one foot in front of the other.

Nothing could be worse than him.

*I won't let anything hurt you, Little Bit*, I tell her, forcing myself to be brave.

A lone gas station appears on my left. Mom used to stop there to get us sodas whenever we ventured to the lake. The lights are on, but I don't see any vehicles parked out front. There's no telling if it's even open this late at night. I debate going there, banging on the door and demanding help, but how bizarre would that seem? A frazzled, deranged woman showing up on foot, a crying infant in her arms? I could tell an attendant I've been kept prisoner for months, but what if they don't believe me? They could take Little Bit away from me. After all the times he's taken her from me, I don't think I could bear to be separated from her again.

Being isolated for so long has muddled my brain, dulled my senses. I'm second-guessing everything and everyone. There's only one person in this world I trust completely, and that's Emily.

I must get to her.

The miles between Emily's house and the cabin seem endless on foot. As I get farther away from the forest, I start to worry I won't have enough strength to keep going.

Even though it's late, a few cars zip past me. When I hear the roar of an engine, I crouch down by the roadside, trying to hide myself. I'm afraid every car will be him, racing through the night in search of me. Once again, I consider flagging down help, but the risk of it being him behind the wheel is too high.

The baby cries again as I stumble back to my feet.

*It's okay, Little Bit. We're almost there.*

Finally, I reach the road leading to Emily's house. It's a long stretch, nothing beyond other than the local fire station. The sight of her familiar house fills me with joy; my chest feels like it will burst, and I'm not sure whether it's from gratitude or exhaustion.

Headlights appear behind me. Looking over my shoulder, I see a car coming down the road. I'm mere footsteps away from Emily's front door, but just as I have with every other passing car, I jolt with fear. This time, instead of hiding in the bushes, I keep moving forward. Only a few more seconds, and I'll be with Emily again. Little Bit and I will be safe.

The car picks up speed, the engine growing louder and louder. Part of me thinks I'm paranoid again. It's too dark to see what type of car it is, but if he did wake up to find I was gone, it wouldn't take him long to follow me here.

I mount the porch step and rest the baby's carrier beside the door. My arms ache from exhaustion, relieved to be free from the extra weight. I knock on the door, looking over my shoulder once again.

I hear Emily call "Hello," from inside.

The car is still there, headlights blinding me. I squint to get a better look, and, to my horror, I see his car. I see him.

"Who is it?" Emily says from the other side of the door. I'm so close.

I pound on the door louder, praying Emily will open it. But drawing more attention will put Emily in danger, too. And then what will happen to the baby, to me?

I knock one last time before leaping off the porch. He's so close he almost grabs me, leaving him with a choice. Go after the baby and be seen by whoever opens the door, or chase after me. His mind must be operating as quickly as mine, debating what to do.

I'm on the verge of screaming her name when a hand covers my mouth, stopping me. I feel my body being yanked into the bushes, just before the front door slides open.

It's Emily. She's just as I imagined her, but she looks tired. I watch as she bends down, peering at Little Bit inside her carrier, a look of awe on her face. I'm about to call out to her again when I feel a warm hand wrap around my neck.

"Not a word," he hisses, so low there's no way Emily could hear. He's on top of me in the bushes, holding something sharp against my neck.

I'm too afraid to speak, to move. All I hope is that Emily will take the baby inside and keep her safe; as long as that happens, I don't care what becomes of me.

Emily, her voice raspy and choked, says to the baby, "You're going to be okay." The sound of her voice brings tears to my eyes, even as I fear I'm seeing her, seeing my daughter, for the last time.

His hand is over my mouth. The blade is pressed against my throat. I catch one more glimpse of the door as it closes, imagine Little Bit with Emily on the other side, before he drags me away.

# FORTY-FOUR
## EMILY

The forest zooms past me as I speed down the highway.

I check my phone every few seconds, waiting for service bars to appear. Finally, I'm close enough to town to make a call. My first instinct is to call the police, but I hesitate.

Despite the horrible scene I found in the attic, I'm still no closer to finding Erin. Everything I've uncovered is circumstantial. All I know is that Viv and Matt own the house by the lake and it appears someone was being kept there against their will. Still, there's no solid proof that person is Erin. The only thing I know for certain is that I broke into my friends' vacation home. I need answers to my burning questions before turning to the police. That, and I can't stand being away from Rosie another second.

I also don't want to risk the police arriving at Viv's house before me. She doesn't need to learn the truth of her husband's betrayal from strangers. She should hear it from me. I'm still struggling to process how Matt could have been behind all this, how he could have developed a secret affair with my sister and fathered a love child. Viv will be absolutely devastated.

Another possibility shakes me to my core. What if Matt arrives at the house and sees Rosie? Since she was left on my doorstep, he hasn't been around her unless I was in the room, too. If Rosie is his child, he might use this opportunity to take her and skip town. I can't let that happen.

If I involve the police now, they'll ask questions, demand truth. I can't let anything, even their assistance, delay me from reaching Rosie. I push harder on the gas pedal, whip out my phone and call Byron instead.

"Emily?" He picks up on the second ring. "What's wrong?"

He must hear my labored breathing. I realize I'm crying, too. Tears rolling down my face and falling from my chin.

"It was Matt," I tell him. The right words don't exist to soften the blow. "He did this to her."

Byron's stunned silence speaks volumes. I hear his sharp intake of breath. "What do you mean, 'It was Matt'?"

Everything comes thundering out at once, each sentence falling into the next. I tell him about the photograph I found, the cabin, the bed in the attic with a chain attached to the headboard. Between my crying and rushed speech, it's difficult to take a breath. Byron remains silent, listening.

"Where are you now?" he asks.

"Driving to Viv's house."

"No," he says, forcefully. "Don't go there by yourself. Get the police involved."

"Rosie is there!" I shriek in desperation. No one, not even the police, can protect her the way I can. I don't want to delay being near her even for a second. "Besides, Matt is at the office. Viv is there alone, and she needs to know the truth."

Byron sighs. He's clearly not impressed with my train of thought, but that's nothing new. I hear rapid movement on the other end of the line, jangling keys. "I'm coming to meet you."

"Thank you," I say, dropping the phone in the passenger

seat. I press my foot harder against the gas pedal, the remaining miles feeling endless.

The gate is already open when we approach. My stomach tangles in knots. As desperate as I am to reach Rosie, I don't want to confront the reality of what I've uncovered. I don't want to tell my best friend that her husband is a liar, a cheater. I still can't wrap my mind around the fact Matt was behind all this.

And what exactly did he do with my sister? Did he kill her after Rosie was born? Was he too overwhelmed caring for Rosie on his own, and that's why he left her on my doorstep?

The car screeches into park. I hurry across the courtyard and burst through the front door. Viv and Rosie are in the living room. Viv's elbow is raised, holding a bottle to Rosie's mouth.

"I didn't think you'd be back so soon." Her cheery expression falls when she sees my face. "What's wrong? Did the police find something?"

"I didn't go to the police station."

My adrenaline is in overdrive. All I want to do is grab Rosie and rush out of the house, get away from Matt's world as soon as possible, but I force myself to remain calm. Viv doesn't know what I know. What I'm about to tell her will rock her world to its very core.

I sit beside her, relief washing over me when I see Rosie. My eyes scan their living room for what feels like the first time, taking in every detail and comparing it to the rugged cabin down the road, comparing the man I thought I knew to the evil betrayer he actually is.

"Do you know about the cabin by the lake?" I begin, unsure of how ignorant she is about everything.

"Our cabin?" She seems confused. "Yes. What about it?"

"I didn't know you had one," I say.

Viv rolls her eyes. "It was a stupid investment. I can't even remember the last time I went up there. Matt put it on the market ages ago."

That's what he told her to keep her away. Viv thinks the place is in the process of being sold.

"A police tip put the cabin on my radar. I didn't even know it belonged to you," I say. "That's where I've been. I broke in—"

"You broke in? To our cabin?"

"Please, listen," I say, putting my hand over hers. "When I went into the attic, I found handcuffs and chains. Someone was being kept there against their will."

Viv's face turns pale. She blinks. "I don't understand."

My heart aches, having to break down every detail for her. "I believe Matt and Erin were having an affair. I think he was keeping her hostage in the cabin by the lake." My eyes skim over Rosie. "I think he's the father of her baby."

Viv snaps her head back, taking a better look at the child in her arms. "That doesn't make sense. He wouldn't—"

"Think of everything Adam said," I say. "That Erin was in a relationship with someone she couldn't tell me about. She was ashamed. I kept trying to think of who that person might be. One of her exes. I even suspected Byron. Matt would fit the bill, too."

"He wouldn't do that to me," she says, her pitch climbing. "He wouldn't do that to you! Kidnap your sister?"

"I wouldn't believe it either," I say, my mind conjuring images of what I saw, "if I hadn't seen those chains. How do you explain that?"

Viv breaks. I'm not sure which detail startled her, which detail rang true. Tears fill her eyes, and when she tries to speak, her voice is ragged. "Maybe there's a reasonable explanation."

"Maybe," I say, squeezing her hand tighter. "But we can't risk being around him until we know for sure."

She nods, her tears landing on Rosie's blanket. "We should call the police."

I wrap my arms around her, no word or action enough to

provide the comfort she needs. I can't imagine how difficult it is for her to turn her back on Matt, but it's the right thing to do.

"Let me grab Rosie's things," I say. "We can go straight to the police station. Tell them everything."

"Okay." She clears her throat, her voice growing stronger. "What do you need me to do?"

"Keep feeding her," I say, wanting to keep her focused, calm. "All I need are bottles and formula. There's already a diaper bag in the car."

I hurry into the kitchen, my adrenaline from earlier returned. Breaking the news to Viv was excruciating, but the hard part is over. Once the police know the truth, maybe we'll finally find out what happened to Erin.

Rosie begins to cry. Viv starts singing to try and soothe her, but it doesn't help. I imagine the baby is picking up on our own emotional intensity.

"Everything's going to be okay," Viv coos. "Don't you worry, Little Bit."

That name makes me freeze. I've heard it before, but in the chaos of the moment, I can't remember where.

"What did you say?"

"Just a little nickname I made up," Viv calls from the other room. "Why?"

"It's nothing," I say, trying to focus.

Little Bit. That's what I used to call Erin when she was a baby. It's been so long, I'd forgotten. What are the chances Viv would come up with the same nickname?

There's a line of bottles drying on the counter. I swipe my arm around them, sliding them into a bag. Looking through the window over the sink, I see another car has arrived. The sight of it makes my stomach plummet. It's Matt's car. My blood runs cold.

"Viv!" I call out to warn her, but before I have the chance to say anything else, I hear movement behind me.

Viv is here, standing beside me in the kitchen. Rosie is no longer in her arms. Instead, she holds a heavy wooden rolling pin she must have palmed from one of the nearby counters.

Before I have a chance to ask what's happening, a sharp pain strikes the top of my head, and the world turns black.

# FORTY-FIVE

The pounding in my head wakes me. I clench my eyes tighter, trying to squeeze the pain away, but my memories make that impossible. Those empty cuffs in the cabin by the lake. Viv holding Rosie in her arms, calling her Little Bit. Matt's car in the driveway.

Viv attacking me with the wooden rolling pin. The throbbing pain is endless.

I sit up, realizing the room around me is almost completely dark, save for a small lamp in the far corner of the room. Heaps of furniture draped in white linen look like ghosts of various sizes waiting to greet me. It's quiet. To my left, a rough wooden staircase rises to meet a door. This must be the basement. In all the times I've visited their house, I've never been here.

"Emily?"

I jump at the sound of my name. I'd assumed I was alone. Icy fear spreads through my body as I turn around, dreading whatever Matt and Viv have in store for me.

The person staring back at me isn't who I was expecting.

It's Erin. At least, I think it's her. Her eyes and features are undeniable, but everything else is unrecognizable. Her hair is a stringy, matted mess. Her skin is ashen and sallow. She looks like she's lost weight. She steps closer, wiping her eyes with her knuckles like she can't quite believe what she's seeing.

"Is it really you?" she asks.

Her voice is recognizable now, indisputable. Hearing it, after more than a year without her, makes something inside of me break. I rush toward her. She doesn't have time to brace for impact, my embrace so strong it almost knocks her back on the bed.

"I can't believe it's you," I say, my throat raw.

Erin pulls back, staring at me.

"You shouldn't be here," she tells me. "It isn't safe."

My lungs feel like they can't get enough air. I stare at Erin, each blink seeming like it will erase her forever. I can't believe she's here in front of me. I can't believe she's alive. And I can't believe *she's* trying to protect *me* from danger.

"Have you been here this whole time?" I ask her, one of the hundreds of questions thundering through my brain.

Erin shakes her head, opening and closing her mouth like she's afraid to speak. Tears well in her eyes, and I'm unsure if it's emotion from seeing me again or fear.

"How did you find me?" she asks.

"I never stopped looking for you," I say. Shame fills me, as I realize for a big part of this year, I believed she was dead. Still, I stalked Adam, vowed to do whatever it took to find out what had happened to her. All that searching led me to the cabin, which eventually brought me here. "After Rosie turned up on my doorstep, I had even more reason to keep looking."

"Rosie?" She looks confused.

An embarrassed titter escapes my lips. "The baby. That's what we've been calling her."

"Oh." She laughs nervously. "Does that mean you know... everything?"

I feel like I don't know anything other than the fact she's

alive, which is enough. She raises her hand to tuck a strand of hair behind her ear, and I see a glint of metal. She's handcuffed to one of the exposed metal pipes, just like she was back at the lake house.

"He keeps the key over there," she says, pointing to a hook near the staircase.

In his rush to bring me down here, he didn't have time to tie me up. Who knows if he even has another set of restraints? I grab the keys, my fingers fumbling to turn the lock as soon as possible. When the handcuffs pop open, my body floods with relief.

Erin rubs her hands gratefully. Red marks circle her wrist. The sight of them makes me nauseous.

"I found a picture of you and traced it to the cabin through a tip that came into the police hotline. I broke in and found out the place belonged to Matt. I came straight here because I needed to get Rosie and warn Viv." Betrayal cuts through me, stealing what little strength I have left. "I didn't realize she was involved."

Erin's lips form a straight line. It's as though she dreads the sound of their names. "I've seen her since I've been here. She knew where I was being kept this entire time. She wanted the baby for herself."

A small part of me knew something was wrong when I heard her say Little Bit. My memory went straight to Erin. Viv must have heard her use the name, or maybe Matt picked it up. I just didn't want to believe that, on top of everything else, my best friend could do this.

I squeeze Erin's hand, trying to let her know that I'm here for her. "What have they been doing to you?"

"I don't know where to start."

"How about the beginning?"

Her eyes fill with tears again as she tells me everything. How she ended up sleeping with Matt after a holiday party. She swore it was a mistake and would never happen again, but then it did. I never would have pictured the two of them together.

She explains, "The longer we were together, I saw just how complicated his relationship with Viv really was. They haven't been happy for years. The only reason they stay married is for the business. You'd never guess that by watching them around the office."

She's right. I've seen them outside the office, too. Viv and Matt appear as much in love now as they did over a decade ago, when they first started dating. It pains me how much Erin sounds like a clichéd mistress, inventing scenarios to justify her decisions, but now isn't the time to take her to task. I need to know how we ended up here.

"The whole time you were gone, I thought Adam was to blame," I say. "When he showed up at the restaurant, I assumed you'd gotten back together."

She shakes her head. "We were only friends. Being in a relationship with Matt meant I had to keep a distance from everyone else who knew us both. Adam was one of the only people I could trust."

She couldn't tell me about the affair. I think of all the times I confronted Adam and accused him of being a controlling boyfriend. He insisted that their relationship was platonic, but I didn't believe him. Now Erin's telling me the same thing.

"Adam agreed to take me to the train station so I could leave town," she says. "And then Matt showed up. I never turned off the location sharing on my phone."

She explains that Matt begged her not to leave. He promised that he still wanted a life with her, he just needed a little more time. He planned to leave Viv for good, and they could start a family. Together.

All that changed once he had her at the cabin. Her body stiffens as she recounts her memories, still painful all these months later.

"He told me his plan."

"Plan?"

"He said that he'd finally told Viv about the affair. That I was pregnant. That I'd been staying with him in the cabin," she says. She begins to cry harder. "He said that the crux of their marriage issues was the fact she couldn't get pregnant. Telling her about the baby had brought them closer. They wanted to raise the baby together. My baby."

"What the hell?"

"He kept telling me how the baby would have a better life with Viv and him. That I wasn't ready to have a child. And even though I was angry, I knew they were right. I thought maybe I could do it with Matt by my side." She pauses. "But he made it pretty clear he didn't want that anymore."

"Did you agree to give them your baby?"

"I'm not sure what I agreed to do anymore," she says. "A small part of me thought maybe the baby would be better off with him, away from me. It had been months since I'd talked to anyone. Matt was the only person I had contact with, and he had turned on me. I had no way of getting in touch with anyone else."

"They set it up that way," I say.

I can't imagine my sister's strange predicament over the past year, blocked off from the outside world and everyone she knew. Matt had become her only access to food, water, socialization. It's understandable that whatever he told her she'd take as gospel.

"Then the baby was born," she says. "I was so disconnected from everything. I didn't even name her. I called her Little Bit. And that overwhelming feeling of holding her in my arms for the first time changed everything. I had a child. And she needed to be protected. I knew that instinctively, but I was weak. My mind and body were fighting to recover. Matt started visiting more often, and when he left, he'd take Little Bit with him.

Never for too long, of course. He'd take the baby back to Viv, then bring her back to me to feed."

I try to imagine the unbelievable scenario. The horror and pain and risk associated with giving birth by herself, only to immediately go into mothering mode. I related to that experience, in some ways. I was overwhelmed with the urge to protect Rosie from the moment I laid eyes on her, before I even knew she was related to Erin. Once I knew the truth, that Rosie was a part of my sister, part of me, that sensation only grew.

I imagine how gut-wrenching it must have been for Erin when Matt took the baby away. The fear she must have felt, knowing that she might never see her daughter again.

And then she tells me about the night she escaped, trekking all those miles in the dark to my house, leaving Rosie on my doorstep. I can't believe she was so close to me that night, just by the path, Matt holding a switchblade to her throat.

The portraits she paints of Viv and Matt are terrifying. To think they'd been keeping her hidden all this time, locked away in a cabin in the middle of the woods, that they were trying to steal her baby.

My chest swells with emotion. Part of me wishes Erin would have flagged down help before she got to me. But I realize how psychologically damaged she must have been. She'd been cut off from the rest of the world for an entire year. The thought of walking into the nearest gas station and reporting Matt's crimes must have been overwhelming.

"Why did they bring you here instead of going back to the cabin?" I ask.

She shrugs. "I think they were afraid I might escape again, or that another driver might have seen me walking along the road." She closes her eyes. "If I'm right here with them, it's easier to finish their plan."

"What plan?"

"They won't need me forever," she says, her voice shaking.

"They've only kept me around this long to feed her, but she's older now. Almost six months." She pauses. "Viv wants me gone. I've heard them arguing about it. She's ready for this to be over, especially now that everyone knows about the baby."

"You're still alive," I say, still trying to comfort her. "I'm with you now."

"Matt keeps making excuses not to hurt me," she says. "But I think he's running out of time. And there's no telling what they'll do now that you're here."

I narrow my eyes. "I don't care what they have planned. We'll find a way through this."

"How?"

Truthfully, I have no idea, but I'm not going to tell her that and risk destroying what little hope she has left. "I called Byron on my way here and told him the cabin belongs to Matt. At the very least, he'll start getting worried when he doesn't hear from me."

Erin's eyes grow wide. "What about the baby?"

Before she can answer, the sound of keys captures our attention. A door creaks open, the sound prompting me to move closer to Erin, to protect her. I've done my best to tell her everything will be okay, but the reality is, we're in huge danger. I have no idea how we're supposed to get out of this.

Matt appears on the staircase, the sight of him knotting a lump of dread in my chest.

# FORTY-SIX

Next to me, Erin freezes, her fear controlling her every movement. She stares at the stairwell, wide-eyed.

"It's okay," I tell her, holding a finger to my lips, begging her to be quiet, her panic causing her to hyperventilate.

Matt comes closer. Seeing him in the flesh, after hearing everything Erin had to tell me, unleashes a fury I didn't know existed. I step forward.

"What the hell is wrong with you?" I shout at him. Erin tugs on my arms, holding me back. "What were you thinking?"

Matt, never one to handle a situation on his own, looks frightened. His hands begin to shake. He looks between Erin and me, his face filled with shame.

"I can explain—"

"It's too late," I tell him. "Whatever you're thinking about saying, this has to end. You can't keep us here any longer."

Matt starts breathing heavier. His eyes twitch, as though struggling to keep up with his thoughts. His mouth opens and closes, debating on what to say, but Erin beats him to it.

"Is the baby safe?"

"The baby..." He stumbles over his words. "She's with Viv."

"Is she the one who hit me over the head?" I ask. "Or was it you?"

"It was me," he says, cowardly. "I didn't know what else to do! I came home and heard everything you were saying to her. You knew about the cabin. About everything we'd done."

"I still don't understand," I say. The more I can keep him talking, the longer Erin and I will be safe.

"Viv is willing to forgive me for the affair, but only if we keep the baby."

"What was your plan? You couldn't start walking around with a child and not expect people to ask questions."

"We'd eventually tell people we decided to adopt," he says. "It wasn't much of a plan. We were figuring it out as we went along."

"And what were you planning to do with me?" Erin asks. The hollowness of her words penetrates me. "I thought you loved me."

Matt stares at her, unable to speak.

He must know that there's no way out now, for either of them, but he's desperate.

"I never intended for any of this to happen," he says, refusing to meet our eyes. "There's no other option anymore. Now that the world knows about Rosie, we can't keep her unless you're never found."

They're going to kill her. It's the only way they can keep their crimes hidden from the public. It must have been part of their plan all along, but the realization is sickening now, having them both so close to me, the history between them amounting to nothing more than death and destruction. Familiar possibilities flash through my mind—Erin being strangled, beaten, her body abandoned some place never to be found—except this time, instead of Adam committing these crimes, it's Matt. And Viv. My best friend is conspiring with her husband to kill my sister.

Matt cuts his eyes at me, his stare making my blood run cold. "Both of you can never be found."

I realize my fate is now tied to hers. If they want to continue their charade of a happy marriage, if they want to keep Rosie, both of us will have to die. I imagine how Erin's story will continue to unfold in the following months. Erin March, never found. Her sister dying tragically in the wake of her loss, leaving her generous, wealthy friends to care for little Rosie. I feel as though I might be sick.

"Matt, you can't be serious," I say, conjuring all the emotions from our decade of friendship into my voice. "Viv would never let you—"

"Viv is the one who sent me down here." It's the strongest his voice has been this entire conversation. "It's her way of punishing me for what I did." He clenches his eyes shut, as though speaking to himself. "I never should have cheated on her. Gotten another woman pregnant." When he opens his eyes again, there's clarity in his stare. Understanding. "This is the only way to make things right."

I'm prepared to keep pleading with him, but I'm stunned into silence when I see him reach into his jacket and take out a knife. I wonder if it's the same weapon he held against my sister's neck. Erin takes a step forward, spreading her arms in front of me.

"Emily doesn't deserve this," she says. "She didn't do anything wrong."

"She broke into our cabin," he says. "She figured everything out."

"And can you blame her?" Erin says, still walking forward.

I'm amazed that after everything she's been through she can remain so calm when facing her captor. I can't look anywhere but at the knife. When I dare to raise my gaze, though, I see something. Someone. We're no longer alone in the basement. Another person is creeping down the staircase.

"You know what it's like to love someone," Erin says, still walking toward him. I realize she's distracting him, trying to stop him from turning around. "Maybe you feel that way about Vivienne. Maybe you felt that way about me once."

Matt cups his chin with his other hand, trying not to cry. "I didn't want it to come to this."

Behind him, I watch as the person descends the stairs. My heart bursts with gratitude when I see it's Byron. He must have rushed over after my phone call. Now he's here, coming to our rescue in silence.

"You can still change your mind," Erin says, her voice steady, focused. "Think about the baby."

"I am," Matt declares, his tone changing. "I'm doing this for her."

In the next second, he raises his arm, ready to strike. He's too late. Byron swings, clocking him on the side of his head with his fist. The hit takes Matt by surprise, knocking him off balance. The knife falls from his hands, skidding across the cement floor.

Erin and I jump back, speechless. I'm about to help when Matt comes back swinging, landing a heavy punch in Byron's gut. The two of them continue swapping punches. I'm astounded by the violence in front of me as the two men beat each other. Part of me wants to get involved, try to help Byron, but every time I do, he gets another hit in, stunning Matt.

Eventually, they wrestle to the floor. Byron manages to land on top of him, holding him in place. Something shiny captures my attention. I bend down and retrieve the handcuffs I took off Erin, passing them off to Byron. Another struggle ensues as he tries to close the cuff around Matt's wrist, but he finally does. I move forward then, holding his other arm back to give Byron the advantage. With both his arms pinned down, Byron manages to attach the other half of the handcuffs to the pipe Erin was tethered to moments ago.

Matt howls in defeat. "Stop! Please! You can't do this to me!"

Erin steps forward now, bending down in front of him. The irony is astounding. Matt must feel so weak right now, so help-less. It's only a fraction of what my sister must have been feeling for the past year.

"You told me you loved me. That you wanted us to be together. You took me to the cabin and promised we were going to start a new life," she says, her voice wavering. "Instead, you locked me up. You lied about me to the rest of the world. And you took my baby from me."

"You don't understand," he says. "Viv—"

"You had a choice," she interrupts, her voice growing in strength. "Every day you continued to make that choice. For an entire year. You deserve everything that's going to happen to you."

She turns to look at me. Already, I sense some of her strength is coming back. She stands taller, shoulders back. The helpless woman she's been forced to be is shedding away.

Byron, still out of breath from the fight, leans his head against the wall. "I saw Matt's car outside and got scared. The front door was wide open, like he'd rushed in, and then I heard voices."

"What about Viv?" Byron doesn't yet know about her involvement, that she's just as dangerous as her husband. "Didn't you see her?"

He shakes his head. "I'll wait here with Matt. My phone is in the car. You need to call the police."

"I have to find Rosie! She isn't safe with Viv." I turn to look at Erin. "You should wait with them. You'll need medical assistance."

But she's already walking past me. "I'm not staying here one more second. I want my baby."

I'm in no position to argue with her, and every moment is precious. "We'll call the police as soon as Rosie's safe."

Byron nods, his eyes locking on mine, begging me to be careful. I head for the door, daring one more look at Matt before I leave.

"I'm sorry," he says to Erin.

She doesn't give him the courtesy of a response before dashing up the stairs in search of her child.

# FORTY-SEVEN

There's no one on the first floor. I thunder up the stairs, going into the first room on the left because the door is cracked. The sight of the room startles me. The walls are painted ballerina pink. There's a mural of dancing white bears on the wall, stars sprinkled around their heads like a halo. There's a crib and a rocking chair. Baby books and toys. Viv and Matt have created an entire nursery in their house. The reality of what they planned on doing, keeping Erin's baby as their own, sinks further in.

"What the hell?" Erin says behind me, looking at the room with disgust.

"Don't worry about this," I say, pressing past her to get back in the hallway. "We have to find them."

My spirits sink further as I search the other upstairs rooms, leaving their bedroom to last. The bed is made, the room immaculate. If Viv has run, it doesn't look she's taken anything. Then again, what would she want? Rosie is all that matters; everything else can be replaced.

A sound from outside catches my attention. I approach the large window that overlooks the backyard. That's when I see them. Viv is swaying in the large swing beneath the gazebo, Rosie in her arms.

I squeeze Erin's forearm. "They're outside."

We stumble down the stairs we'd just climbed, hurrying to get to the backyard.

The sound of the French doors opening gets Viv's attention. "Back so soon?" she says, smiling. Only then does she raise her head to see it isn't Matt who has returned, it's me. And I'm not alone. She stares at Erin, as though she's seen a ghost.

"Erin?" Her voice shakes.

"Give me the baby," she says, marching forward. I hold her back. I'm afraid of what Erin might do to Viv. Worse, I'm afraid of what Viv will do to Rosie. She holds her closer to her chest, protectively.

I recoil at the sight of her. I still can't believe my best friend is behind all this, has been lying to me, torturing me for the past year. My mouth is dry when I begin to speak.

"Matt told us everything. He said you're the one who wanted to keep Rosie."

Viv's wild eyes bounce between us. "Where is Matt—"

"Matt said you wanted to keep Rosie for yourself," Erin cuts her off. "You're the reason he kept me a prisoner in that cabin."

Viv appears frozen, her trance breaking when she looks at the baby. "Please, don't do this. We never wanted to hurt anyone."

"You have hurt people," I tell her. "I've been mourning the loss of my sister for a year. You watched me suffer, all the while knowing where she was. You watched my marriage fall apart. And what about Adam?"

"What about him?" Erin looks at me, alarmed. In the chaos, I haven't told her what happened to him, the one person who tried to help her.

"Someone killed him," I tell her. Erin raises a shaking hand to her face. I look at Viv. "I'm guessing Matt did that, too."

Viv shakes her head. "Matt was following you. That's how we knew you weren't with the police. You were really meeting with Adam. After you came home, I went to his apartment. I thought if something happened to him, maybe the police would become suspicious of you, and you wouldn't be able to keep the baby."

"And you were just going to swoop in and take her?" I ask. "And frame me for murder?"

Viv shakes her head again. "We can give her a better life, don't you see? Matt and I have everything." She looks at Rosie. "Except this. And it's the one thing we didn't have that tore us apart. He started to resent me. Had an affair." She cuts venomous eyes at Erin.

"I'm sorry, Viv," Erin says, weakly.

"Shut up!" Viv screams. She jerks her arms so violently, I worry for Rosie's safety. "Don't you see everything you've taken from me? That all the people who've been hurt were hurt as a result of *your* actions?"

I sense some part of Erin believes this. It's the reason she remained docile all this time. She considered it her penance, feeling she deserved to have her life taken away.

But Rosie doesn't deserve any of this. Viv must see that.

"You've been taking care of Rosie all this time," I say, trying to remind her of what's important.

"Her name is Madilynn," she says. "And I've been with her since the night she was born. I've taken care of her. Loved her. She's *my* child. We only took her back to the cabin so Erin could feed her."

"You must have known this couldn't go on forever," I tell her. "Rosie, or Madilynn, would wean eventually. And then you'd just have a woman locked up in your vacation home."

"We should have gotten rid of her weeks ago," Viv says, her furious stare locked on Erin. "Matt kept stalling. If we'd ended it before she had the chance to escape, none of this would have happened."

They planned to kill Erin. It's the only way they could have concealed all their crimes. They kept her alive during the pregnancy and needed her to feed Rosie in those early months. Still, they could have killed her at any time. Maybe Matt did have feelings for Erin, and that's why he couldn't go through with it.

"You'd have to explain how you got a child." The words escape before I can stop them. Clearly, Viv is unhinged enough to not be thinking clearly, but part of me wants to know how they really thought they could get away with this.

"It's easy when you have money," she says. "That was the whole plan behind the Denver office. We could go to a new location. Start over."

They were biding their time, waiting to move across the country and start anew. It's terrifying to think how close they came. The only thing connecting them to any of this was the tip about the cabin and the picture I found in Erin's belongings. If she hadn't managed to escape, they could have moved and taken Rosie with them. And then what would have happened to my sister?

"I understand that feeling," Erin says, stepping forward. "You want to believe everything is going to work out. That's how I felt when I first went to the cabin. I thought Matt and I would be together with the baby. That's the lie he told me to keep me there."

"Matt isn't lying to me," she says, defensively. "He did all this *for* me."

"Matt's lying is what led to this in the first place," I say. "You can't really think you can move on. This will follow you wherever you go. Rosie deserves more than to be raised by a liar and a cheater."

"And a killer," Erin adds under her breath.

That last word wounds Viv more than all the others, as though she's only just realized how low she's fallen. Her desire to become a mother and hide her husband's affair has cost her everything. Her closest friend, her soul. And now she's going to lose Rosie too, a child who should never have been hers to begin with. She appears lost in thought, staring at Rosie. She doesn't notice Erin inching closer.

"I see how much you love her," I tell Viv. "How you were willing to do anything to protect her. Right now, what's best is keeping her safe. You still want to do that, don't you?"

"I can keep her safe!" Viv shouts, her volume startling the baby. Rosie begins writhing in a frenzy.

"It's okay," Viv says to her, trying to calm her. She stares at the baby in her arms, tears trailing down her cheeks. It's as though the only thing that exists in the entire world is this child —Madilynn—and the life she envisioned for the two of them.

Erin is close enough now that she could reach out and grab Rosie, but she's afraid. Viv's unpredictable, and we don't want to do anything that could hurt her.

I step forward. Viv is now sandwiched between us, still lost in her own emotional turmoil. Erin reaches forward and snatches Rosie at the same time as I grab Viv's hands, forcing them to let go.

Viv struggles against me, but I use all the strength I have to hold her still. Erin slides the baby from her arms, starts running toward the house.

"Please!" Viv shouts after her. "Don't do this!"

She turns aggressive, trying to push past me to follow them, but I keep her in place. As she fights against me, we both fall to the ground. The pain I feel doesn't matter; I can't let her get close to Erin and the baby again.

"Stop, Viv," I say, weak and out of breath. "Just do the right thing."

Viv collapses, falling into tears. Part of me wants to comfort her, as I have so many times before, but I'm well aware of how dangerous she is, how much heartache she's already caused. I position myself so that she can't get away easily, should she catch a second wind and start fighting again.

"What do I do?" Erin shouts. I realize she's still in the backyard, watching in horror as I wrestle with Viv on the ground.

I reach into my jacket and pull out my phone, toss it to her.

"Call the police," I say. "Tell them what's going on."

She starts to dial the number, then pauses, staring ahead. I can only imagine what she's feeling.

"You can do this," I tell her. "Hurry."

She presses another button and holds the phone to her ear. Another wave of relief comes when I hear her speak.

"I need to report a kidnapping," she says. A few more seconds pass, and then I hear her say, "My name?"

A pause, momentary fear freezing her into silence. She's about to become real again. My sister is back, and it's time the rest of the world found out. I imagine the person on the other end of the call, their mouth dropping open when Erin reveals she's the girl who was missing, presumed dead.

She takes a deep breath and says, "My name is Erin March."

# FORTY-EIGHT

Only one police car arrived at first, but now dozens of vehicles are here. The only thing keeping the media from storming the grounds is the private gate at the front.

Everything has snowballed. I can only imagine how Marco and the others at the newspaper will react when they get all the details.

Adam's murder. Erin's imprisonment. Viv and Matt's lurid scheme to kidnap Rosie and raise her as their own. At what point their crimes would have stopped remains a mystery. They would have murdered Erin, hidden her body. I would never have known what happened to her.

Police and medics swarm her, asking questions and checking her vitals. She sits in the back of an ambulance, preparing to be transported to a nearby hospital. Rosie is in the ambulance beside her, about to take the same journey.

Even though I can't stop thinking about Rosie, I stay with Erin. It must be killing her to be away from her child, even though she knows she's safe. She's staring to her left, I think trying to catch a glimpse of Rosie. Then I see she's staring at something else. The police cruiser. Viv sits in the back seat.

"I still can't believe any of this is real," she says. "A big part of me believed I'd never leave that cabin alive."

An even bigger part of me thought the same thing. That I'd never get to my sister again. The appearance of her child changed that, but I still wondered if we'd ever make it to this point, where we're all safe.

"It's almost over," I tell her. "Don't waste your thoughts on them."

Erin continues staring. "Maybe Vivienne is right," she says. "You saw that nursery up there. This house. All the money from the business. They'd be able to a provide a better life for the baby than I could have ever dreamed of."

"That's not true—"

"Yes, it is," Erin says, cutting me off. "Look at the way we grew up. Mom wasn't a good parent. What if I end up just like her?"

I squeeze her hand. "The way we were raised wasn't easy, but we got through it. Together. We can do the same thing now."

Erin looks down, wiping a tear from her cheek. "Everything is already so messed up. Look at all I've put her through."

"She won't know about any of it," I tell her. "She's still a baby. All she's going to remember is that she has people in her life who love her."

The cruiser begins to drive away, taking Viv out of our lives forever. I never could have imagined she'd be behind all of this. That she could be capable of hurting my sister or me so deeply. My eyes brim with tears at the realization of everything I've lost.

"You really think I can do this?" Erin asks me. There are tears in her eyes, too, reminding me, despite Viv's betrayal, of everything I've gained. My sister. My niece. Family.

"I know you can," I say, pulling her into an embrace.

# FORTY-NINE

Six Months Later

I pull up next to the curb, watching flakes of snow fall on the windshield. I've always loved the beauty of winter, especially when it can be enjoyed from the cozy warmth of my car.

Erin exits the brownstone and walks over. She slumps into the passenger seat and lets out an exhausted sigh.

"How much longer am I going to have to keep doing this?" she asks.

"I think that's a question for your therapist," I say. "You complain about having to go to the sessions, but aren't they helping?"

"I complain about going anywhere in this weather," she says, staring at the sludge accumulating beneath the wipers.

It's funny how an innocuous phrase like this, something about the weather, will take my mind back. I think about what last December was like, when I was desperate and grieving the loss of my sister. I imagine her holidays alone and chained to a bed inside her lover's vacation home. We never thought we'd end up here. Together again.

"I'm starving," she says, kicking her feet onto the dashboard. "Let's get going."

Some things never change. As easily as my mind can go back to the sad moments of our past, I'm just as easily reminded how each day is bringing us closer to normalcy, even if things will never be the same as they once were.

Erin is in bi-weekly therapy, has been ever since she returned. She complains about the hassle, but we both know the sessions are working. She has an unbelievable amount of trauma to work through, and as overwhelming as it might feel at times, I'm confident in the people she has around her.

Thanks to resources set aside by various victims' charities, Erin hasn't had to return to work full-time. Just last month, she started working remotely a few hours a week doing customer service. It eases her back into a routine, as well as reacquainting her with small talk among random people, two skills she'll need to master at some point.

The part-time hours allow her to be with Rosie more often.

Rosie. The name seems to have stuck. I often ask Erin what names she considered when she was pregnant, or even in the early weeks after the baby was born, but she insists none of them suited her. I wonder if it wasn't a defense mechanism her mind constructed, a way to protect herself from knowing she would have to give up her child.

That's the reality she was forced to face. That, and the fact her own lover would kill her once she was no longer useful.

Both Matt and Viv are due to go to trial this summer. Despite their fancy defense teams, they're each looking at serving decades in prison. They've been charged with a slew of crimes, from Erin's imprisonment to Rosie's abduction, and, of course, Adam's murder.

There's a knot in my stomach every time I think of Adam. For so long I blamed him for what happened to Erin. I never imagined everything he told me was true, that he'd only been trying to help my sister, a selfless act that he ended up paying for with his life.

Erin doesn't talk about him often, but when she does, it's always happy memories. She truly believes she would have been in more trouble if he hadn't tried to help her. Once a month, she visits his grave with a fresh bouquet of flowers.

We pull into my driveway and sit in the car in silence, watching as more snow falls around us.

"I've been looking at apartments," she says.

"Have you?" Erin rarely leaves the house. She's only driven a few times since she was freed, hence why I take her to and from her therapy appointments.

"I mean, I've been looking online," she says. "I'm keeping my promise to be out by January."

I shake my head. Erin and Rosie have been living with us, and even though she insists we need space, I know she isn't ready yet. Or maybe, I'm the one who isn't ready. After so many months without her, having her this close is comforting, not smothering.

"Let's just focus on the holidays," I say. "One step at a time."

Erin fixes me with a look before getting out of the car. "Trust me, you and Little Bit are going to need the room."

The beloved nickname no longer refers to Rosie. I look down at my growing stomach. I'm already feeling swollen and exhausted. I can only imagine how I'll feel once the third trimester comes along.

We walk inside the house, the scent of cinnamon sticks and pine peppering the air. Byron is in the kitchen, wearing a ridiculous holiday-themed apron. I come up behind him and he leans back to kiss my cheek.

There was a point in time when I never thought we'd get back here. Suspicion and resentment formed a barricade between us, especially since I accused him of being involved with Erin's disappearance. Now, I know it was only my own desperation making me paranoid. Byron was always doing what he thought would be best for me, whether it was encouraging me to value the other parts of my life or investigating Erin's case on his own. He was there for both of us on that final day, overpowering Matt so that we could escape and find Rosie. He's forgiven me for all the pain I've put him through, a testament to how much he truly loves me and this life we're building together.

Rosie sits in the jumper hanging in the doorway, kicking her feet wildly. She starts smiling and babbling when she spots Erin.

"Mama's home," she says, going over to her daughter and scooping her up.

As happy as I am to have my sister back, there's nothing more heartwarming than watching her become a parent. It's a full circle moment. When I was a child, I bit off more than I could chew caring for Erin. It was a responsibility I carried with me the rest of my life. I still carry it. She might have made mistakes, but all those lessons prepared her to become the best mother possible. I only hope, in a few months' time, I can adapt as naturally as she has.

We've both become the versions of ourselves we truly needed to be. Erin with her newfound maturity, putting her healing and her daughter first, while I've learned to take a step back, to appreciate people and situations for what they are. It was a long, tumultuous road to get here, but I wouldn't trade our situation for anything in the world.

"Is the snow starting to lay?" Byron asks, turning around to kiss my cheek. I peek over his shoulder to see what's on the stove. Vegetable soup. The aroma makes me salivate.

"Starting to," I say. "Looks like we'll be working from home in the morning."

"My favorite type of work day," he says, returning his attention to the pan.

Now that Viv and Matt's company is for sale, I returned to journalism. Marco couldn't get me my old position, but Byron's publication was happy to make room. Some people say it isn't wise to work alongside your partner—Viv and Matt used to say it all the time, not that their opinions matter—but I've found it nice having the extra quality time together, especially in the wake of all the time we missed.

"Are we going to put up the Christmas tree or what?" Erin says, resting Rosie on her hip.

"Come on," I say. "I'm exhausted."

Erin points at the window. "It's snowing outside. There isn't a better time. Besides, this is Rosie's first Christmas. I'm ready to celebrate."

Rosie smiles adorably, making it hard to say no.

"Fine," I say, walking toward the garage. "I'll start getting out the boxes."

"We'll help," Erin says, as she carries Rosie behind me.

Once again, I'm overwhelmed by how lucky I am to be in this position, one I thought I'd lost forever. I've found my family again, even if it looks different than before.

In my eyes, it's better than ever.

# A LETTER FROM MIRANDA

Dear reader,

Thank you for taking the time to read *The Baby on My Doorstep*. If you liked it and want information about upcoming releases, sign up with the following link. Your email address will never be shared and you can unsubscribe at any time.

*www.bookouture.com/miranda-smith*

As dramatic as certain elements of this story may seem, it's, unfortunately, rooted in very real scenarios. In the past, I've read about infants being abandoned in public, or even at private residences, and wondered how life unfolded for everyone involved. The baby. The biological parents. The courageous bystanders willing to render care. Sometimes I find it empowering to take back control of situations I can't understand through my writing, and that's what I aimed to do with this story.

If you'd like to discuss any of my books, I'd love to connect! You can find me on Facebook, TikTok and Instagram. If you enjoyed *The Baby on My Doorstep*, I'd appreciate it if you left a review. It only takes a few minutes and does wonders in helping readers discover my books for the first time.

Thank you again for your support!

Sincerely,

Miranda Smith

facebook.com/MirandaSmithAuthor

instagram.com/mirandasmithwriter

tiktok.com/@mirandasmithwriter

# ACKNOWLEDGMENTS

There's a huge team of people I'd like to thank for their help on this project, the most important being my editor, Ruth Tross. Your suggestions made this story stronger and more emotional. Thank you.

I'd also like to thank the other talented members of the Bookouture team, including Kim Nash, Sarah Hardy, Jane Eastgate and Liz Hurst.

To my family, thank you for your endless support and encouragement. Much love to Harrison, Lucy and Christopher. This book is dedicated to my sister, Whitney. It's been so rewarding watching you settle into motherhood. I'm happy we get to raise our children together and take on all sorts of adventures!

As always, thank you to the readers for taking a chance on this book. It's because of you I get to do what I love for a living. I'm forever grateful.

# PUBLISHING TEAM

**Turning a manuscript into a book requires the efforts of many people. The publishing team at Bookouture would like to acknowledge everyone who contributed to this publication.**

### Audio
Alba Proko
Melissa Tran
Sinead O'Connor

### Commercial
Lauren Morrissette
Hannah Richmond
Imogen Allport

### Cover design
Lisa Horton

### Data and analysis
Mark Alder
Mohamed Bussuri

### Editorial
Ruth Tross
Sinead O'Connor

**RAISING READERS**
Books Build Bright Futures

Dear Reader,

We'd love your attention for one more page to tell you about the crisis in children's reading, and what we can all do.

Studies have shown that reading for fun is the **single biggest predictor of a child's future life chances** – more than family circumstance, parents' educational background or income. It improves academic results, mental health, wealth, communication skills, ambition and happiness.

The number of children reading for fun is in rapid decline. Young people have a lot of competition for their time, and a worryingly high number do not have a single book at home.

Hachette works extensively with schools, libraries and literacy charities, but here are some ways we can all raise more readers:

- Reading to children for just 10 minutes a day makes a difference
- Don't give up if children aren't regular readers – there will be books for them!

- Visit bookshops and libraries to get recommendations
- Encourage them to listen to audiobooks
- Support school libraries
- Give books as gifts

There's a lot more information about how to encourage children to read on our websites: **www.RaisingReaders.co.uk** and **www.JoinRaisingReaders.com**.

Thank you for reading.

hachette
UK

Printed in Dunstable, United Kingdom